Because We Are

Mildred Pitts Walter

Lothrop, Lee & Shepard Books

NEW YORK

Because We Are

Mildred Pitts Walter

Library of Congress Cataloging in Publication Data

Walter, Mildred Pitts.
Because we are.

Summary: After a misunderstanding with a white teacher, black honor student
Emma is transferred from the integrated high school where she has excelled to
a segregated school where she finds a different kind of challenge.
[1. School stories.   2. Afro-Americans—Fiction.
3. Race relations—Fiction] I. Title.
PZ7.W17125Be 1983   [Fic]   83-987
ISBN 0-688-02287-1

First Edition

1   2   3   4   5   6   7   8   9   10

Text design by Lynn Braswell

To my young friends:
Brenda, Craig, Eric, Jerry,
Jill, John, Lloyd, Michele,
Ronald, Ruby, Sheryl, and Vinita

One

A Santa Ana wind blew in from the San Gabriel Mountains. The grounds at Marlborough High School were deserted that hot October noonday as Emma made her way toward the cafeteria. She moved quickly, a smile on her face, feeling pleased with herself. She had just been told she had been elected to the National Honor Society. Everything was falling into place. A scholarship to a major university would surely come; the words *Emma Walsh, M.D.* flashed in her mind, and now the Golden Slippers would certainly want her as a debutante. She felt a sudden rush of excitement. Did she really want to be a deb? Don't be silly, she told herself. Who wouldn't want to be a Golden Slipper deb?

Should she break the news to her friends now, or just let it filter through the grapevine? Would the news that had made her so happy become another achievement for which she might have to apologize? Maybe she would tell Cheryl and Dee.

Inside the cool room, she paused to let her eyes adjust to the change in light. Marvin called to her, "Hey, Em, over here."

As always she sensed that special joy on seeing him and the pleasure of being with friends in that section of the cafeteria where the Blacks gathered for lunch. She hurried through the hash line and started toward Marvin and her friends.

She passed those on the fringe of the main group. There was boisterous laughter; some people were practicing new dance steps around a group playing cards. "Hi, beautiful lady," a boy shouted at Emma.

"Beautiful?" muttered a girl whom Emma recognized from her English Composition class. "Better say 'white-girl lady.' " There was a burst of laughter.

Emma burned with shame and anger, but pretended she had not heard. It was well known that she maintained a four-point grade average, was the only Black on the student council, and that she had white friends. Would she forever have to prove her Blackness?

She placed her tray on the table where Marvin

was seated with her main friends, Cheryl and Dee.

"Get up, Melanie, so Emma can sit next to Marvin," Dee demanded.

"You don't belong at this table anyway," Cheryl said.

"I belong wherever I want to be," Melanie replied defensively. She left and began table hopping to prove her point that she moved back and forth between the groups.

Emma squeezed in beside Marvin. He kissed her cheek and grinned. "How's my woman?" he asked close to her ear.

Her skin prickled with delight, but, also, she felt a rush of shame. She hated his showing affection in front of everybody, even though he was a great basketball player, the school's hero—Marvelous Marv.

"Can't you see? She's *fine,* man." Everybody laughed at Ron, a cello player, the only Black in the school orchestra. The laughter at her table, everybody in their section talking at once, the handslapping—all the body language—made her feel warm, safe, at home.

Then "white-girl lady" flashed in her mind, and she recalled that last year when she first joined Marvin at that table, all talking had stopped. She had not been welcomed there, either. "Oreo chick" they had named her. But with a few phrases at the right times in the right places, Emma had gradually proved her right to belong. On second thought she decided not to mention the National Honor Society award to anyone.

Marvin held his sandwich for her to take a bite. She accepted. He grinned at her and she settled comfortably to eat her lunch, again pleased with herself. Then she saw Ms. Simmons. The young English teacher had red hair coiled around her head; and her skin, too fair by California standards, was sprinkled with freckles. Emma caught Ms. Simmons' eye and saw a look of surprise.

"Emma Walsh!" Ms. Simmons called, then made her way toward the table.

"Your shadow, Emma," Dee whispered.

"The long *white* shadow," Cheryl muttered, and there was a burst of laughter.

Ms. Simmons ignored the laughter. "There's student council next period. I'd like to see you there." She looked from one group to the next with obvious disapproval. "I hope we don't lose her to you people."

There was silence at Emma's table. Emma felt anger rise in her. *What the devil is she trying to pull? Acting like we're close—in front of my friends, yet.* "What do you mean 'lose' me?" Emma asked.

Ms. Simmons smiled. "Just want you to know we need you, Emma." She went on her way.

Emma sat feeling the old shame and humiliation Ms. Simmons had a way of arousing in her. The mood at the table was poisoned, and Emma knew that the effects would spread beyond these cafeteria walls.

Reluctantly Emma left Cheryl and Dee at the table. Marvin's parting words whispered in her ear were: "OK, baby, get on. It's your being white time now." She laughed. He should have to deal with student council, she thought, especially Danny. She hoped Danny would not be there today, slinging his long blond hair, telling his jokes and trying to impress her with his familiarity with "ghetto talk."

The student council hall was alive with laughter when Emma arrived. Danny was there, as usual the center of attention. When Danny saw Emma, he shouted, "Hey, Karen, here's your *best* resource." Turning to Emma, he said, "Karen has to write a paper about welfare. Why don't you help her out?"

"Why do you think I can help her?" Emma asked.

"Don't all y'all know 'bout welfare?"

Everybody laughed. Emma looked at Ms. Simmons. Ms. Simmons smiled and said, "All right, let's calm down so we can get to work; and remember we're lucky to have Emma. I was just reminding Emma that we need her. She's not only smart, but she's pretty, too."

How could Ms. Simmons let Danny get away with that? Why does she have to always make me out so different? Get hold, Emma told herself, but she didn't have to take that. She smiled sweetly, bowed her head, and said, "Thank you, Ms. Simmons." Then she walked out of the room, and slammed the door.

At seventh period, in Ms. Simmons' English Composition class, Emma found students around the teacher's desk, handing in papers. "Oh, my goodness," she cried. What with a science report, extra math, and a history test, she had forgotten to do the assigned outline. She rushed to her seat to get something on paper. Too late. Ms. Simmons was up and down the aisles now, collecting papers.

"Ms. Walsh?"

Ms. Walsh? I'm in trouble, Emma thought. She's gone all formal: "Just one minute, Ms. Simmons," Emma pleaded.

Ms. Simmons stood by Emma's desk. "You can't make it on past performance, you know. I am disappointed in you, Emma. You have great potential."

"You don't know me," Emma said without looking up.

"I know you've done excellent work heretofore, and with your background—"

"You don't know a thing about me, my potential, *or* my background, so . . . just forget it." Emma tried to control her anger. "I'll turn in the outline before the day is over, OK?"

Ms. Simmons flushed under her freckles, patted the coil on her head, then pressed her hands on Emma's desk. "You *are* an outstanding student; you have leadership ability. You could be in the mainstream, Emma."

Emma glanced at the other Black in her class, the one who had called her the "white-girl lady." Suddenly there was the moment with Ms. Simmons in the cafeteria and again in the council hall—that humiliation. She straightened her back and turned her head sharply away from Ms. Simmons, her lips pouting.

Ms. Simmons continued angrily, "I can get you into the mainstream, but I can't keep you there. *You have to want to be there.* I know your parents don't approve of you isolating yourself with hall walkers . . . with riffraff."

"Don't be calling my friends riffraff," Emma exploded.

Ms. Simmons hesitated, then put her hand on Emma's shoulder. Emma shoved her hand away. "Don't touch me, white witch."

Ms. Simmons' face was paler than ever now. "Go to the office and wait until I come."

Emma, stunned, at first could not connect the idea of motion with her body.

"I said get out of here." Ms. Simmons ground the words between her teeth, almost in a whisper.

Emma stumbled out into the hall, knowing she was in trouble.

Mrs. Phillips, the girls' vice-principal, was standing in the doorway of her inner office, talking to the secretary and school nurse, when Emma entered.

"Why, hello, Emma," Mrs. Phillips said. "Congratulations. Ladies, I'll have you know you're looking at one of our National Honor students. Isn't she terrific?"

Emma smiled weakly.

"What can I do for you, Emma?" Mrs. Phillips asked.

Should she tell Mrs. Phillips what had happened now, or should she wait until Ms. Simmons could hear all that was said? She decided to say only, "Ms. Simmons asked me to wait here for her."

"All right. Sit in my office. I was heading down the hall; I'll be right back."

Emma waited, trying to ignore the rising fear. Suppose they expel me? They couldn't. Not for that, she told herself. She knew she was an "opportunity transfer" student, living out of Marlborough's district. For the least mistake, she could be out. The shame and humiliation, now mixed with fear, was worse than anything she had ever felt. What would her mother say?

It was not long before Mrs. Phillips returned with Ms. Simmons. "Emma, Ms. Simmons tells me something very hard for me to believe. Is it true?"

Emma sensed imminent danger and felt cold inside. "I don't know if it's true or not. What did she tell you?"

"You attacked her and cursed her in front of the class."

"I did not!" The words rushed out.

"You most certainly did!" Ms. Simmons countered. "And not only that, she's been most hostile recently—a chip on her shoulder. She stormed out of council meeting today for no reason at all."

"How can you say I had no reason when you agreed with Danny that I was the best resource on *welfare*?"

"I never agreed with Danny. Remember? I reminded them that we're lucky to have you. And you walked out."

"Well . . . Emma, we are lucky to have you," Mrs. Phillips said. "You're smart and attractive—"

"You see?" Ms. Simmons interrupted.

Emma's first impulse was to laugh, but she knew if she started, she'd never stop. Stay cool, she told herself. The room was silent. Finally, Emma said, "But I didn't attack you. I pushed your hand away, and I'm sorry. . . ." Emma stopped, trying to control the rising tears.

"Being sorry is not enough," Ms. Simmons said angrily.

"What you've done is very serious, Emma," Mrs. Phillips said. "You could be arrested for attacking a teacher, you know that? But I'm going to let you go home."

"Go home?" Emma cried. "If to apologize is not enough, what *can* I do? I'll do anything, Mrs. Phillips, but I can't go home."

"Under any circumstances, we'll have to talk to your parents before final decisions are made. Your parents are divorced, aren't they?"

Emma dropped her head.

"Your mother can come alone," Mrs. Phillips said.

"Please, don't bring my mother into this. I have just one more semester after this one, and I'll be gone from here. Can't we settle this, Ms. Simmons?"

Ms. Simmons did not respond. Emma looked at Mrs. Phillips. "Please, can't we?"

Mrs. Phillips sighed. "I have a thousand students here to think about. Can you imagine what would happen, Emma, if they all got it into their heads to act the way you did today? I cannot bend the rules. Not for you, not for anyone. We'll see what happens after we talk to your mother."

Emma sensed that all her dreams were dying; her world was falling apart. Marvin! She must tell Marvin. But the next moment she found herself running . . . running home.

Two

*Emma heard her bedroom door open slowly. She pre-*tended she was asleep. She could not face her mother and go over all that again. Soon the front door closed; the car started, and she knew her mother was off to see about getting her back into school.

What a stupid thing to have done. The election to the National Honor Society and the possibility of becoming a debutante were now dimmed by her foolish action. Why did I let her upset me, make me lose my cool, when so much was at stake? Why had Ms. Simmons lied? And pretending all this time I was one of her favorite people. In desolation and fear, Emma knew she was in this all alone.

The little clock near her bed said ten o'clock. She

kicked off the light-green blanket and got up. In her
closet she found a pink cotton robe, worn and soft.
Now it was too long for short and too short for
long, but she put it on.

With the drapes and curtains drawn to keep out
the heat that the persistent Santa Ana winds brought,
the house was dark.

In the kitchen she turned on the fire under the
kettle and went on to the bathroom. Bright tile and
sparkling bowl reminded her of her mother's need to
have things just so. She felt a pang of guilt: a senior
getting into that kind of trouble.

As she showered, she found herself trying to push
away the thought that she might be expelled. But it
didn't work. The worry was only followed by the
fear that the Golden Slippers Social Club might
reject her as a debutante. What if she had to leave
Marlborough and her friends there? The thought of
trying to make new ones overwhelmed her. It had
taken two years and a lot of effort to win those few
friends at Marlborough. And not seeing Marvin everyday would be unbearable, too. She saw him now
as she always saw him in her mind's eye: tall, lean,
bronze, up and down the basketball court, smooth as
silk, making baskets effortlessly. What would happen to their relationship if she were not there?
They'll let me come back, she told herself. Ma'll
convince them.

Making toast and hot chocolate occupied her for

a while, but then she was not hungry; the fullness was all the way into her throat. She felt she was alone against a wall of darkness. The kitchen, her favorite room, with plants crowding in from the ceiling did not cheer her. At times she had laughed when her mother talked to those plants as if they were children. Now she wished she were on speaking terms with them. Why didn't her mother come?

Finally she heard the key in the lock.

"Well, you've blown it this time," her mother said angrily. "Emma, how could you, after all I've been through for you? Hitting and cursing a teacher!"

"I didn't curse her."

"Whether you called her a bitch or not is of little importance. The fact that you put yourself in a position to be accused *is*."

"Ma—"

"No!" her mother interrupted. "You listen to me. They told me how, here lately, you have been isolating yourself with the Black kids; and how you don't participate in school activities the way you once did."

Emma looked at her mother. She felt as though the dark wall was closing in.

"Why do you Black kids feel that you have to bunch up together?" She waited.

Emma said nothing.

"Emma, I send you to a mixed school to learn all

you can learn. Then you go there and segregate yourself. Why do you feel that you have to segregate yourself?"

"I don't. Mama, you don't understand that teacher."

"That teacher only wants what's best for you."

How can that teacher know what's best for me? exploded in Emma's head, but she said nothing.

The doorbell rang. "That's probably your father. Let him in."

Oh, *no,* Emma thought. Oh, God, please don't let Jody be with him. A flash of Jody's light-brown hair and big gray eyes reminded Emma that Jody was friendly, but a stranger, nevertheless. And what with being white, she was likely to remain a stranger. But her father had every right to bring Jody if he liked. After all, she was his wife and had been for the last three years, ever since Emma was fourteen years old.

"Girl, let your father in," her mother said.

Her father strode in alone, his tall frame slightly stooped, looking more uncomfortable than usual. He hated discussing things with her mother.

"Sit down, Larry," said her mother. "Would you like some coffee?"

Emma had come to know that tense tenderness in her mother's voice.

Had her mother never really stopped loving her father? Had she still not forgiven him for leaving them right when he had begun to achieve some success as a doctor?

"No, thanks. I just had breakfast. What was decided about Emma?"

"They're transferring her," her mother said. "Sending her to Manning. It's just our luck that we live on the very edge of Manning's district. Unfortunately, Manning is her home school."

Emma felt the shock of both relief and pain. She was not expelled, but her chance of becoming a debutante was narrowing. What would she do without her friends? She would surely lose Marvin, being that far away. She shivered.

"Manning?" her father asked. "Surely there are other schools. What about Fairmount?"

"I've pulled all the strings we know to get them to let her return to Marlborough, or send her to another integrated school. But Emma has not been the most cooperative recently. We're lucky. They could have expelled her. She's going to Manning unless she can finish this year in a private school."

"You have the money for that?" her father asked.

"Where you think *I* get the money?" her mother demanded. "We're hardly making it on my salary. You know how much social workers make. And that chintzy three hundred a month you give—only fifty more than the courts mandate—doesn't go very far."

"I just can't afford the extra expense of private school."

Her mother jumped up and stood in front of Emma's father. Even though he was sitting, she looked small and terribly helpless, but she lashed out,

"You can afford a nonworking wife, a Mercedes for yourself *and* your wife; and marina fees for that boat —*Jody's Joy*. But your daughter? Don't you care anything about Emma?"

"Of course I care! But private schooling is out of the question."

Emma wanted to scream, Stop it! She didn't want them fighting. Why couldn't they think of her and how she felt? Just this once.

Her father went on, "It might do her good to go to Manning. Maybe she'll learn there what we've been trying to teach her: All this Black togetherness is no solution."

They're miles apart on everything, she thought, but they're in agreement against me. How could she explain to them the shame and humiliation Ms. Simmons made her feel? *Me and my friends don't segregate ourselves; we're segregated.* How could she make them see what was happening to her? She didn't know herself why she felt so much better when she sat at the tables with other Blacks. She just knew she needed the warmth that being with them gave her.

"Furthermore," her father said, "even if money were available, it would be foolish to start her in private school in her senior year. I'll take care of her debut, and if she graduates, then I'll see to it that she goes to college."

If she graduates. Emma heard little more. She knew she had to face the consequences of being transferred and make the most of it.

Three

The car horn sounded again. Mama's patience was
already thin this early in the morning. If only there
was another way to get to Manning, Emma thought.
With no direct public transportation from Brandon
Heights to school, Emma's mother delivered her
every morning before work and picked her up after
school on the way home.

The horn blasted. Emma grabbed her books,
dashed out, and climbed into the backseat.

"Get up front," her mother said.

"Mama, its too uncomfortable up there. You have
the seat right up to the dash. I can't help it if I have
Daddy's long legs."

"And his bad disposition? I see why you're making me late. All that makeup. Wipe it off."

"Aw, Mama, you should see what the other girls wear!"

"You don't need all that stuff on you."

"If I take off any of it, I'll feel naked."

"Look at your eyes. Girl, you'll blind yourself."

Emma let out a deep sigh, trying to control the rising anger. What was wrong with her mother? Lately she's treating me like a ten-year-old, Emma thought, and here I am going to be eighteen soon.

"Come on, wipe it off!"

"Thought you were in such a hurry." Emma squeezed in up front and flipped down the visor to look into the mirror. "Go on! Start the car. I'll do it."

She removed some of the makeup, and tried to tuck her long legs more comfortably into the small space. She looked out at the fast-receding palm trees and wished she was heading for Marlborough. There she had friends to share all her moods, especially Marvin. But she didn't want to think about Marvin. She thought of Allan Page Davis, the one steady friend she had gained at Manning. For two weeks now she and Allan together had waited each morning for the crowd to arrive.

Her mother looked at her and smiled. "You look much better, fresh and pretty. Too bad soft lovely skin is wasted on silly girls who don't know how to appreciate it."

Are all mamas like her? Emma wondered. She never finds anything pleasant to say any more. Can't she see how cramped up I am? No, she has to check me out. She sighed and looked at her mother. The round face with smooth dark skin, resigned in a kind of sadness, was beautiful. But she's so tense, Emma thought. "Ma," Emma asked, "why you worry so much?"

"Ha!" It sounded as though her mother had been waiting for the question. "When you're a woman, you'll understand."

"I *am* a woman."

"Uh-huh. . . ." Her mother kept her eyes straight ahead. The sadness on her face deepened.

Emma shifted on the seat. Why can't she give Daddy up? she thought.

The car pulled alongside the curb in front of the school. Taking her time, Emma unfolded herself out of the car and reached into the back for her things.

"Emma, please . . ."

". . . don't keep me waiting after school." Emma finished the sentence.

"You're so smart. See if you're smart enough to keep out of trouble. You're here by the grace of God and my goodness. Not many mothers would drive way over here every morning before work. Remember that."

"Yes, Ma, I'll remember."

She walked toward the auditorium steps, knowing that her lips were pouting. Allan Page was waiting. How glad she was that he was somewhat shy, not aggressive like Marvin. He always seemed to know when she had gone the rounds with her mother and needed time to erase the frown from her forehead and the pout from her lips.

How pleased she was that he was there. She recalled her first day at Manning when he had walked up and told her his name. "You look so scared. Don't be. I'll help you, if you let me." He became her ace, her very special friend.

Over the weeks, as they waited for the crowd to arrive, they had shared bits and pieces; but she had never told him why she came all the way across town to Manning. He knew she was a science major, interested in medicine; that she had a very special boyfriend at Marlborough High; and he knew about her stepmother, too. She knew his mother had lost her job as a school cafeteria worker because she could not pass the written test, and that his father was dead.

As she approached, he smiled his slow, easy smile and said, "It's a good morning, eh?"

She sighed. "Oh, man. I can't deal with my mother. Git sick of her lip. But I shouldn't say that. She has it pretty tough. It's a drag driving way over here every day."

"I've been wondering why you come way over here. Can't be an opportunity transfer. Not from Marlborough to Manning." He laughed.

"Could be," she said matter-of-factly.

"But not likely," he said.

Silence floated between them. She was glad that he did not pursue the question. She took out her makeup kit and began replacing her makeup.

"Why put all that goop on your face?" Allan asked.

"You sound just like my mama," Emma retorted.

"With skin like wild honey, you don't need it. You're a pretty lady."

She opened her lively, bright brown eyes wide and brushed on mascara carefully. She touched her fingertip to her tongue, then smoothed her eyebrows. She looked at Allan and winked. "My friends at Marlborough like my makeup."

"Hey," Allan said excitedly, "now I'll get a chance to meet those friends at the big game, eh?"

"Yeah. They'll be here, and Marlborough will be state champions, what you bet?"

"That's not even a bet, woman," Allan said and laughed.

"We'll see," Emma said and blotted her lipstick.

The crowd was arriving now. Emma remembered her first day at Manning. Right off she noticed the absence of white students. With the exception of a few Asians, Chicanos, and Mexican-Americans, the student body was Black. The discovery was a pleasant shock. At Marlborough, Blacks had been few. Emma had known and related, in some way, to all of them. It was impossible to get to know half the people on this campus.

The crowd thickened. Each group stood off by itself. Blacks split into many small groups.

"These people you see in and out of the building before the bell are the *boojeis*," Allan said.

"Boojeis?"

"The well-to-doers, the rulers, functionaries, police people."

"Oh, you mean the bourgeois."

"Right. On campus over there, that's Carrie and her entourage, the *climbers*—the want-to-be rulers; and to my right holding forth, is Brenda, a typical *survivor*."

"Who's the stout girl she's talking to?"

"That's Liz. They're all rough—trying to make it."

Emma was surprised that he thought that way about students. Allan went on. "Then there are the *toms*, laughing at demeaning jokes or begging for attention at any cost."

"Which one are you?" Emma asked.

"I'm a loner, swimming against the tide. I observe."

"I can't say I'm a loner, but it looks as though newcomers are no more welcomed here than they are at Marlborough."

In every group, excitement about the football championship game between Manning and Marlborough dominated the conversation. Emma, on the fringe, longed for her old friends and wondered if she would ever be a part of any of these groups.

The bell rang. She gathered her things and said to Allan, "Stay for lunch today."

"Oh-h-h, no! I'm going home."

"Please, Allan. I just hate eating alone. Stay."

"First place, I don't have any money. I can't take that long line and ole Eoil Can and his friends."

"Eoil Can. Who's Eoil Can?"

"Haven't you met Eoil Can, the thief? You will."

Strange one, that Allan. Smart, too, Emma thought as she made her way to first period. This was also Allan's senior year. He had gone to Bel Air in the volunteer free busing programs for elementary and junior high students. He could have gone to any high school in the city on a volunteer transfer, but he had chosen Manning. Why? she asked herself as she hurried down the hall.

The morning passed quickly. When the bell rang for fifth period, Emma rushed to the cafeteria, thankful she had homeroom just before lunch. The informal atmosphere made it possible to be at the door ready to make that mad dash to avoid the long lines. With less than a thousand seats in the cafeteria for two thousand students, lunchtime at Manning became a true test of "survival of the fittest." Fifth period was the best, sixth not so bad, but seventh was impossible. She hoped she would never have seventh period for lunch.

Emma was among the first to finish eating. She

waded through the groups and on to the outside. The line waiting to get in was still long and the grounds seethed with others eating lunch from bags. She saw several members of her science class under the bonsai tree, gazing at the sky. As she approached them she noticed one of them was holding a watch. She stood near, but they paid her no attention.

Suddenly someone shouted, "They're here."

"Right on the minute," the timekeeper said.

Then Emma saw a flock of sea gulls heading in like raiders. Students tried to take cover, but there was no place to go as the crying gulls came to feed, raining their droppings, flapping their wide wings, their beady eyes alert, their yellow beaks ready.

A great commotion spread through the crowd and then a scream, "He took my sandwich."

The scrawny bird, with the whole sandwich in its beak, soared away. It was done so quickly, Emma hardly had time to see that the sludge-colored bird was small for a mature sea gull. Its feathers were scarce and scattered, its eyes exposed beads, and its beak rough.

"Ole Eoil Can did it again," someone shouted and the crowd laughed.

So that was Eoil Can, Emma thought. A survivor. Evidently, the gull had lived through an oil slick and was making it. The other gulls settled and fed as familiars. The crowd took its usual form. Suddenly Emma felt a tap on her shoulder. "Can't y' say 'hi' t' people?"

Emma looked around. There was Liz. Short, stout Liz, whom Allan had often called rough. "Oh, hi," Emma said, surprised. She had seen Liz often in that group teasing Allan. No one in that group had ever spoken to her.

Liz smiled, but Emma noticed that even though the smile seemed warm, it did not soften her black eyes. Could Liz be deceptively mild?

"I've been watchin' y' every mornin' with Allan. What y' name?"

"Emma. Emma Walsh."

"I know y' friend done told y' who I am. Where's he?"

"He went home for lunch."

"Pretty outfit y' got on there. You dress good, y' know." Liz reached out and touched the soft wool of Emma's sweater.

Emma felt her face going hot. She was not accustomed to strangers being so direct. Her friends at Marlborough knew clothes meant little to her, and what she was wearing today was not fine at all.

"Come over here with me. Want y' t' meet my friends," Liz said.

Emma followed Liz toward a group of girls who looked her up and down as she approached. Suddenly she felt as though she had been recruited and Liz had been ordered to escort her into camp. Some stares were openly hostile, but Liz's directness had offered Emma a challenge. She pushed through the loud, boisterous crowd and was finally encircled by

Liz's friends. Liz did the introductions. There was silence. Emma realized that she had not encountered girls exactly like these before.

Then Brenda, who had appeared the most hostile, said, "Y' from the hills, eh?"

"I live in Brandon Heights," Emma said.

The bell rang.

"I thought so, with your saddity self." Brenda walked around Emma and the group laughed.

The words hit Emma like a sharp and chilly wave. I'm not stuck-up, or grand, either, Emma thought, but said nothing. That Brenda could be a problem she really did not need. She started toward her class. The chill of Brenda's words did not go away. Emma felt she was right back where she had been at Marlborough High when she was trying to erase the image of "Oreo chick." But she was in no mood to prove anything to anyone. She hadn't sought them out, she told herself, even though she had met them willingly enough. What would Allan say? She had been jammed by the *survivors*.

Four

The stadium hummed with a thousand voices that cool, sunny November afternoon. Pre-game pep cheers flowed in waves. All day the campus had been poised, shrouded with a particular hush, a suspense —waiting for this moment to release the outburst that would sweep Manning to victory over Marlborough, making Manning city-wide football champions.

The boojeis were in command, leading the cheers:

> FI-RE-UP, TIGERS, FI-RE-UP
> FI-RE-UP, TIGERS, FI-RE UP
> FIREUP TO FIGHT
> FIREUP TO WIN

Emma, excited by the bustle, pushed through the crowd to find Allan Page. Would he be waiting as he promised? Marvin was coming to the game. She hoped that he and Allan would get on fine. But would they?

The rivalry between Manning and Marlborough was fierce and the city championship game was just the monster to stir tensions that bordered on enmity. Even the strongest bonds could be loosed in the course of a shared sports event. They'll like each other, she reassured herself.

Finally she saw Allan near the stadium. He was desperately trying to reach some girl, who had from behind placed her hands over his eyes. As Emma came closer, she recognized the girl, Brenda. Liz and Brenda's other friends were around Allan, laughing.

"Thank goodness, you're here," Emma said as she walked up.

"Oh, so that's who y' waitin' for," Brenda said, removing her hands. "No wonder y' can't sit with us. Brandon Heights gits all y' attention."

"I'm not even going to the game. I already know the winning team, so why waste my money?"

"Don't be jivin' us. We know where y' comin' from." Brenda and her friends walked away without saying hello to Emma.

Emma's attention was on the crowd. Where was

Marvin? she wondered. Had she missed him? She hoped he hadn't gone into the stands.

"They're on your case, I see," Allan said.

"Who? What you talking about?"

"Brenda and her little crowd."

"Oh. *Them.* I told you Liz singled me out. What are they supposed to be? Tough or something?"

Allan laughed. "They survive."

Finally Emma saw Marvin. Her heart pounded and her insides seemed to do a flip-flop.

"Hey, man!" Allan rushed toward Marvin.

"What you say!" Marvin reached for Allan.

"You two know each other?" Emma asked.

"We're old junior-high buddies," Marvin said, and in the next breath to Allan, "You know this lady?" He took Emma's hand and drew her to him.

"Allan Page is my ace, Marv."

"Did she tell you she's my woman?" Marvin asked.

"Aw, Marvin," she said. She was embarrassed, and tried to subdue the joy that flooded her.

"Well, aren't you?" He touched her chin lightly with his fist and smiled. "You'd better be."

"How come you didn't tell me that the city's leading basketball scorer is your ole man?" Allan asked. "Ole Marvelous Marv."

"How could I know you two were tight? We'd better get on to the game."

"I have your ticket, baby," Marvin said to Emma.

"I have my own."

"Well, we have four. Come on, Allan."

"I'm not going."

"Not going?" Marvin asked. "What kind of spirit is that?" He pressed the ticket into Allan's hand.

As they went toward Marlborough's section, Emma walked between them and smiled as they got reacquainted.

"So, Emma's your old lady? I like that, man, really like that. Listen, I'm going on over to my side. We gonna beat you and make you happy while we doing it. Emma, I know *you* aren't coming over."

"No, I'm not, and no offense to Manning, Allan." Then she thought, Will my Marlborough friends think I am still tied to them? She felt a surge of guilt that she was unable to give all of her loyalty to Manning.

Cheryl and Dee ran to hug Emma. "Girl, the cheerleaders here at Manning are *bad,*" Dee said.

"Too bad Marlborough doesn't have a jazzy pep club like that. If they did, I'd try even harder to get in it. How are you, girl?" Cheryl hugged Emma again.

"Hey, look. There's Em. Hi, Em, what's happening?" came from all sides. She was happy to see all the old faces and so pleased that she had been remembered with affection; but suddenly she had a feeling that she wanted Manning to win the game.

From the starting whistle, the game was tough going for Marlborough; but they stayed in there, with cheers giving their team courage. The game was so close and intense the crowd was like a fuse, slowly burning to an explosion.

Emma wanted to talk, but Marvin was too involved with the game to listen.

By halftime, when Manning's band was on the field and the drill team was thrilling the crowd, the score was fourteen to six with Manning in the lead. Marlborough's section was a little subdued, but confident. "We'll come back and beat you, what you bet?" Marvin said to Emma.

Emma was joyful, but a bit disappointed. She had hoped that the victory would be complete at halftime. Now the game could go either way. "I hate to see you lose," she said to Marvin, "but we've got the best team. . . . Hey, you miss me?"

"What kind of question is that? I should ask you that. You seem to be making it fine over here."

"I'm not. It's different. Real different. Nobody but Allan Page makes sense here."

"Just don't let him make too much sense." He looked at her and smiled.

Emma laughed. "You wouldn't be jealous, would you? I know what's happening between you and you-know-who."

"Your grapevine's working, eh? Women . . . just too much."

"I just bet. All girls wanting to make out with Marvelous Marv. Too much, indeed. Ha!"

"Listen, baby, I'm with *you* now. So let's make the most of the day. OK?"

"What'll we do today?"

"Let's just play it by ear. But I do know we'll go back to Marlborough and welcome our team."

"They'll need more than a rousing welcome to raise their spirits when we're through with them."

"Hey, there's a Manning fan in our midst," Marvin shouted. "Shall we kill her?"

Emma's friends all gathered around and chanted: "Beat 'er up, beat 'er up, yea, yea, yea!"

When things had quieted down, Marvin said, "If you brag again, woman, I'll send you over to the other side and leave you there."

"Allan Page is over there."

"He doesn't have my record, remember. Ha, ha, ha!"

"He doesn't have your anything, Marv." She squeezed his hand and settled down to see the outcome of the second half of the game.

It was touch and go! Marlborough scored, but missed the extra point. Marlborough's fans, nevertheless, came alive. The score was now fourteen to twelve, Manning still ahead. Then Manning trapped Marlborough behind Marlborough's goal line, giving Manning two more points. Marlborough could not get going, and for the second time was trapped for a safety. Marvin was demoralized. Manning won the game eighteen to twelve.

The stadium exploded with Manning's fans clapping, stamping and chanting:

CLAP YOUR HANDS. STAMP YOUR FEET.
MANNING'S TIGERS CAN'T BE BEAT!
ANOTHER ONE BITES THE DUST.
ANOTHER ONE BITES THE DUST!

As the crowd moved outside the stadium, Brenda and her group snaked through, chanting:

WATCH OUT, WE'RE HERE.
EVERYBODY, STAND CLEAR.
WE'RE AT THE PEAK
OF OUR WINNING STREAK.
SO, HEY, EVERYBODY, STAND CLEAR!

When Brenda saw Emma, she shouted, "Hey, look at our saddity friend licking Marlborough's wounds."

"Aw, leave her 'lone," Liz said.

"Yeah, she think she too good for Manning. Traitor," another said.

"The way we done kicked Marlborough's ass t'day," Brenda said, "that chick's gotta' be all they say she is: a washed-out Marlborough Oreo."

"O-oo-o, dog 'er, Brenda," the crowd shouted.

The word *Oreo* exploded in Emma's mind and the jeers of the crowd flamed her anger. She moved toward Brenda, tightfisted, ready to fight.

"Emma, what's all this?"

Emma turned and saw her mother. "Come on here, get in the car," her mother said.

"Wait for me, Marvin." Emma followed her

mother. "Mama, that's just some silly girls. I'm with Marvin. We're going over to Marlborough; he'll bring me home later."

"You're getting in this car and going home, Emma."

"But, why? Why can't I go with Marvin?"

"I don't want you out here with all these crazy people."

"I'm *not* with crazy people."

"I saw you, acting like you were brought up in the streets."

"Mama! What are you talking about?"

"Get in that car."

"Mama, please. Let me go."

"Emma, you're going home. Go tell Marvin he can come with us now or he can come by for you later."

"I can't tell him that, Mama."

"Then I'll tell him."

"No! Please."

"Either you do it, or I'll do it."

Emma fought back the tears as she went over to Marvin. "I can't go."

"What? Why not?"

"Mama says no."

"What about you? What do *you* say?"

"Oh, Marv, I want to. I can later if you come by."

"Listen, woman, I came over here to be with you and for us to spend this day together. Now, you make up your mind. I can't come later. Things are happening *now*."

"Oh, Marvin . . . I don't know what to do."

"I can't tell you."

Emma lowered her head and bit her lips, trying to fight back the tears.

"OK, baby." Marvin kissed her on her lowered forehead and walked away to join his friends.

All that had been close and warm was suddenly withdrawn, and she wanted to run after him, away from her mama who shriveled her, treated her like a little child without any will, without feelings. But she just stood there and shivered.

On the way home she sat in the backseat, hanging on, trying to put it out of her mind. She knew if she said one word she would explode. She must not cry.

How could Mama just walk up and decide that I was in the wrong? How can she go on punishing me for one mistake? What is happening to us? Emma felt that she was fighting a shadow. She had to get her mother to trust her again.

Five

Emma went quietly to her room. She lay on her bed fully clothed, trying to contain the anger, to dispel the humiliation; but she could not clear her mind of her mother's words: ". . . acting like somebody brought up in the street." Ms. Simmons' word—*riffraff*—flashed before her mind's eye and she burned with shame. Why had she bothered with Liz and her friends at all? Why had Marvin deserted her? Couldn't he see that she needed him? Tears choked her but would not flow.

Reluctantly she rolled her hair in curlers, thinking that Marvin might come. She tried to get involved in *Essence* magazine, but the words did not make sense. Too much was whirling in her brain: Would she make her debut? What was happening between her and her mother? If only her father were here—had never left home. Things had been a lot better, even until he remarried.

She remembered how, before, he had come to see her often. They went places—to the beach, to San Diego. Always when he brought her home, her mother would have prepared special dishes that Emma's father liked. They all had time together. Emma prolonged that time, showing her father all the things she had accomplished: her test scores, special projects, paintings—anything to hold them together. Then he remarried. It was as if he had died. His visits became further and further apart.

Now, as she looked back over the past few years, she could see how her mother had changed. After the remarriage, at first Emma had given up hope, also, that he would come back. But then she believed that if she made him proud of her, he'd want to come home. She worked even harder then.

That was one reason why she wanted to be a debutante so badly. Her father would certainly take her mother to the ball. That was a family affair: the daughter of Dr. and Mrs. Lawrence Walsh. She would help her mother choose the right dress and makeup; make sure she was as pretty as she could be; and her father would be so pleased he would like both of them.

What if he brought Jody? The thought paralyzed her. How could she stand before all those people and be announced as the daughter of Dr. Lawrence Walsh and Mrs. Janet Roberson Walsh? Everyone would know she had no family. Her father would dance one dance with her, and then all the rest with Jody. How would her mother feel? Why hadn't she thought of her mother's feelings before?

The phone rang and she was startled out of the depressing mood with a hope that it might be Marvin. She waited to be called. When her mother did not come, she slowly undressed for the night.

Later her mother knocked on her door. "Emma. Emma," she called.

Suddenly the anger at her mother returned. She lay quiet and still. Get hold, she told herself, but she could not answer.

"Emma!"

"Yes."

"May I come in?"

Emma angrily turned over on her stomach and pressed her head down on her folded arms, still not answering.

"Emma, are you in there?"

"Come on," Emma finally said.

Her mother entered and sat on the side of the bed. Emma did not look at her.

"I guess you think I'm hard on you, Emma, but I'm only trying to keep you from destroying yourself."

Emma felt the anger move to guilt. She kept her head down.

"Do you want to make your debut, Emma?"

She felt that she deserved to be a debutante. She had worked hard for it. She had maintained a four-point average; she had not only involved herself in community activities, but she had also participated in many extra school activities. Now she did not answer.

"Let's assume you do," her mother went on.

Emma raised her head and looked at her mother. "Does it matter what *I* want? Are they going to let me?"

"We're doing all we can to make sure that you are accepted. But you're going to have to be on your best behavior."

"Mama, I didn't do anything—"

"Emma, you're going to have to learn that you don't have to start the fire to get burned. You always have to protect yourself. Stay away from people like that."

Anger similar to that she had felt at Ms. Simmons stirred in her. "Like what?" she demanded.

"Like they have no sense and no self-respect," her mother said impatiently. "Now I want you to promise me that you will not be bothered with people like those girls."

"I was not with those girls, Mama. Can't you understand?"

"I *understand* that you're already in trouble, Emma. So promise."

Emma sighed and did not respond.

"Is that too much to ask? That you protect yourself?"

"OK, OK, if that's what you want. I'll promise."

"Oh, Emma. . . ." her mother cried and left. The door reopened suddenly and her mother said angrily, "I wish you'd clean that messy room."

Emma buried her head in her pillow to stifle the sobs. What do they want from me? Mama, Ms. Simmons, my friends? She thought of Liz and Brenda—my enemies? She felt torn. Always she was trying to please. For what? If she satisfied her friends, she offended her parents and teachers. What could she do? Suddenly Marvin's words struck her: "What do *you* say?" "What do I say?" she demanded aloud. That was the burning question that she had to answer, but she knew she could not deal with it then.

It was not even eight o'clock, so Emma decided to watch *Masterpiece Theatre* on public TV. When she walked out of her room, she discovered her mother dressed to go out. Then she remembered it was her mother's bridge-game night.

"I'll be at Ethyl's. I left the number right by the phone if you need me. Think you can do without me for a few hours?"

That was her mother's way of making up. Emma responded, "Oh, I guess so."

"You sure, now?" her mother asked.

"You had better go before I change my mind." They both laughed and an uneasy truce was made.

After *Masterpiece Theatre,* Emma flipped the dial, but found nothing to ease her mind. She went to bed.

Around midnight she awoke from troubled sleep, from a bad dream that she could not remember. The house was quiet. The silence was eerie. She got up and looked out her window. A fog had stolen in, so thick she could not see the streetlight near the house. Quietly she opened the door.

The living room light was still on. Her mother had not returned. What would she do if something happened to her mother? Nothing would happen, she reassured herself. November was the month of fog, and her mother was a good driver. Still she worried.

Finally, she heard a car in the driveway and the garage door open and close. Relieved, she sank into sleep before her mother peeped into her room to see if all was well.

Again she awoke from troubled sleep. It was only twenty minutes after three. She got out of bed and looked out her window. The silent, foggy darkness was still there. Feeling lonely, she thought about her father and remembered how, when she was a little girl, she would wake in the night and go to her parents' room. Her father would always let her into their bed on his side. She remembered the warm place and his nice clean smell of soap. She felt the tears in her throat and longed then to go in to her mother and say how sorry she was about everything —especially sorry for them; but she lay on her own bed and listened for the familiar sounds of the night to break through the silence.

The next morning Emma slept late. On awakening, her first impulse was to stay in bed all day, but she knew she should get up and help with the Saturday morning chores. She hurriedly dressed in faded jeans and an old shirt and went through the silent house. Her mother was already out grocery shopping. On the kitchen counter she found waffle batter, a container of frozen strawberries, and a bowl of whipped cream. She was not that hungry, so she put it all in the refrigerator and went back to her room.

Outside her window the fog was losing the battle with the sun. Emma felt it would be a sunny but sad day. She wished Marvin would call. She remembered the first time she met him. It was the summer before she went to Marlborough. They both were enrolled in Camp Brotherhood USA.

That trip to camp was her first time away from home since her father remarried. One morning she was feeling sad and a little guilty about having left her mother alone, so she slipped out of the cabin and walked on a trail nearby, not noticing where she was going. Suddenly she found herself on the ground with this boy sprawled alongside her.

"Why don't you look where you're going?" He pulled Emma to her feet.

"I'm sorry. But I could say the same for you."

"I'm sorry, too," he said. "I wasn't expecting anyone. I run this trail early every morning and there's never anyone here." He awkwardly brushed the dirt off her, then extended his gritty hand. "I'm Marvin Richard."

Emma told him her name and he said, "Does anybody call you Em?"

"No."

He grinned and said, "Hi, Em."

After that she noticed him everyday, but he seemed oblivious of her. He towered over almost everybody there, and all the girls were mad about him, made him the main attraction.

At camp he settled for a girl named Kali with long, brown, straight hair and green eyes. Kali always wore stark white or blazing colors to complement her deep tan. Before the session ended, she and Marvin were constant companions. They had breakfast, lunch, and dinner together. They sat together at the fireside vesper; they held hands during the films; and he walked her to her cabin door.

Then Emma met him again at Marlborough.

"Hey, Em? You're the tall, tan lady that knocked me off my feet at Brotherhood USA, aren't you?"

Then, to her surprise, he asked her to the Heart-to-Heart valentine party on campus.

Now she rummaged through her chest of "symbols of cherished memories" and found the valentine he had given her that day. She recalled the sweet turbulence when he kissed her at that dance, and her heart pounded. She felt a longing, a hunger that could not be appeased with food. She wondered why he had not called.

The doorbell rang. Who could it be? She rushed to the peephole and saw her friends, Cheryl and Dee.

"Where you guys going so early? Come on in," she exclaimed.

"It's not early. We're going shopping," Cheryl said. "Wanta come?"

"Can't, Mama's not home. Come on back. You guys had breakfast?"

"It's lunchtime, girl. We're going to the new mall out on the peninsula for lunch."

"You can have lunch with me."

As she heated the waffle iron, she prepared the strawberries and rewhipped the cream. "What happened at Marlborough after the game yesterday?" she asked.

"It was sad, girl. We didn't stay there long, and Marvin didn't stay as long as we did. Did he come by?" Dee asked.

"No."

"Girl, you better come on back to Marlborough. Marvin is losing his cool. Those white chicks are all over him, and it's turning his head," Cheryl said.

"Emma, who was that fine dude you walked into the stadium with?" Dee asked. "He was with you and Marvin for a while."

"Yeah, he was fine," Cheryl said.

"That's Allan Page Davis." Emma poured batter on the waffle iron.

"Is he nice?" Dee asked.

"Super."

"With a guy like that, I would forget Marvin," Dee said.

"Allan and me? We're not like *that*. No way. Marvin's it."

"Say, I'm having a party during the holidays. I want Allan to come. OK, Emma?" Cheryl asked.

"I'll ask him."

"And I'm having a slumber party next weekend. You'll have to come, Emma," Dee said. "I bet there're a lot of fine dudes over there at Manning. Must be heaven."

"I wouldn't say that. There're the Lizes and the Brendas, too. You saw what happened."

"Aw, *them*. They just wanted to be noticed," Dee said.

"That's what I tried to tell my mother."

"Mothers don't understand nothing," Cheryl said.

"Oh, yes, they do: how to make you miserable. Like I didn't want to ask Melanie to my slumber party. Well, Mother insisted. Just because Melanie's mother is president of Golden Slippers this year, everybody is treating her like she's the first wife of Haile Selassie. I don't want Melanie there," Dee said.

"I'm not sure I should come to your party, Dee," Emma said. "All you guys going to talk about is the deb ball, and I may not be a deb."

"Aw, Emma, don't say that. You gotta be one, and you better come," Dee said.

When they finished lunch, Emma's mother still had not returned. Emma reluctantly said good-bye to her friends. But she had to cut the parting conversation and rush to the ringing telephone.

It was Marvin. He wanted to pick her up that evening for a movie. Would she like to go?

She held her breath to stifle the squeal of delight. She finally composed herself to say softly, "I'd love that. Yes, that will be nice." The day that she had thought would be a total disaster had suddenly become one with the most promising possibilities. Marvin was coming at six-thirty. Maybe she would give her mother a huge surprise: clean her room. Just maybe.

Six

The late fall darkness was descending early. In Emma's living room, the pale-green velvety carpet, vacuumed to perfection, showed streaks of silver in the glow of the lamplight. Pale-green drapes closing in pale-green walls lent a luxurious comfort to the room. How glad Emma was her father had agreed to a settlement that left her and her mother in this nice house.

She tossed her mink-brown leather jacket over a chair and sat, wiggling, trying to settle more comfortably in her tight jeans as she waited for Marvin. She adjusted her belt. "Oh, darn!" She had broken a fingernail. "My longest one," she muttered.

She rushed to her room to try to save it with

Nail-Fix-It. Just as she opened the bottle, Marvin blared his car horn. Startled, she spilled the glue and her fingers all stuck together. "Mama, bring the alcohol, quick. I need it."

"Why doesn't Marvin come in?" her mother asked as she cleaned Emma's fingers with a swab of cotton. "If he had any respect for you, he'd ring the doorbell so you'd know who's calling. Anybody could be out there blowing."

"I know Marvin's horn," Emma said. "Hurry. I'm late."

"If he'd come in, you'd have time to compose yourself."

"Aw, Mama, you must know there're a thousand girls out there who would die for the chance to ring Marvin's doorbell, take him out, and pay his way anywhere. He's picking me up and taking me out. That's respect enough for me."

"Watch it, now. Don't let yourself become accustomed to being so grateful for nothing. You have money in your purse? Change for a phone call?" her mother asked, following Emma.

"Yes." Emma grabbed her jacket and purse, blew her mother a kiss, and dashed out still putting on her jacket.

"Have fun and be in here by midnight," her mother called after her.

The little Scirocco, though more than seven years old, was shining at the curb. Emma was often amused at the amazed look on faces as Marvin's six-foot-six frame unfolded out of the little car. Though Marvin was a bit cramped in it, Emma loved having all the room she needed to stretch her long legs.

"I thought one time there I'd have to go on without you," Marvin said as she scrambled into the car.

"I wasn't *that* long."

"Next time be waiting on the curb."

"No, next time you ring my doorbell." She leaned over and kissed his cheek. The car screeched away from the curb.

"I'm glad you called," she said.

"Did you think I wouldn't?"

"The way you deserted me yesterday, yes."

"I was disappointed in you yesterday. But to show you're forgiven for deserting me, I'm going to let you choose what we'll see tonight—*Superman, Star Wars,* or *Fame.*"

"Suppose I say *Grease*?"

"No, one of those three."

"OK, *Fame.*"

"Aw, Em."

"Well, what did you want to see?"

"*Fame.* Ha, ha, ha. Now, if you're nice, I might take you to a party I'm invited to after the movie."

They were silent as they drove through busy streets to the freeway. Emma glanced at Marvin. His light-blue shirt was open at the collar under a navy cashmere V-neck pullover. His thin gold-chain bracelet shone in the light of the dashboard as he kept his hand steady on the wheel.

Emma let her hand touch his knee. He looked at her and smiled. Her heart pounded and she gave in to the sweet turbulence. With her head resting on the back of the seat, she closed her eyes and let the sheer bliss of being with Marvin course through every inch of her.

They left the movie huddled together, singing in off-key harmony,

> *I'm gonna live forever.*
> *I'm gonna learn how to fly.*
> *I'm gonna make it to heaven . . .*

"You want to learn how to fly?" Marvin asked. "I'll teach you how to fly at this party."

"Oh, so you think I'm nice, eh?"

He looked at her and grinned.

It was not yet nine-thirty, so they had almost three hours before midnight. Marvin drove the winding road up into the New Highland Hills. In the distance the city was aglow. After she had discovered the wonders of heaven at camp, she had often wondered why stars were so hard to see in the city. Now, as she looked upon that dazzling view, she thought, The stars with all their glory are paled by those lights. If only one could have both.

The view ended abruptly and the car dove into a sheltered area of a private parking space made of heavy planks. The house was almost hidden in tangled vines beyond a flight of steps that led down into a ravine. Marvin held Emma's hand as they walked below, singing, "I'm gonna learn how to fly."

The place, although lighted outside, appeared dark and lifeless inside. "You sure there's a party here?" Emma asked.

"I'm sure. And don't flake out now when we get in there, OK?" Marvin rang the doorbell and they waited.

"Try again," Emma said.

"Patience, it'll happen."

When they had waited for what seemed to Emma a long time, Marvin gave two quick rings. Immediately, they were let in. Dim lights softened the all-white room. There still was no sign of a party as a tall young man guided them through to a stairway that led below.

They entered a room and Emma felt as though she had entered a storm. Black, purple, and pink strobe lights distorted images and gave Emma a sensation like that of moving under water.

As her eyes adjusted, she saw two stereos going simultaneously so that at no time would the room be without sound. Even though there was a monitor at the mixer to synchronize light and sound, the lights and music seemed at war.

People stood in small knots around the room, inhaling deeply, then sharing the joint. Some seemed to float and jerk toward her and Marvin with squeals of delight. She suddenly realized that Marvin was being mobbed by his white friends. The odors, the noise, and Marvin's frenzied welcome all heightened her uneasiness, so she sought out a room where she could reassure herself that she looked all right. She took off her fitted jacket and adjusted her silk blouse in her jeans, then stood before a mirror and checked her makeup. Her long, straightened hair, slightly flipped on the end, with bangs across her forehead, was neatly in place. Her brown eyes sparkled. She was pleased with the way she looked, but unhappy with the quivering of her insides. If only there were some other Blacks out there.

"Marvin, I thought you'd never get here. What took you so long?"

Emma heard the soft demanding voice when she reentered the room.

"Maybe the jive-turkey got lost." Emma recognized Danny. Who but Danny, that showoff from Marlborough, would be spouting such outdated talk, Emma thought and laughed.

"He couldn't get lost. He could find my house in his sleep," the girl said.

Who is this girl, holding Marvin around the waist, looking into his face as though she has found answers to all of her questions? Emma wondered. Seeing them, Emma at first felt anger, then she sensed a peculiar shame. She waited.

It was Danny who first noticed Emma in the room. "Well, if it isn't our Emma," he said with exaggerated enthusiasm. "Hey, man," he shouted to Marvin, "how do you rate a chick like this?"

"She's not a *chick,*" Marvin said, pulling Emma into the circle that had mobbed him. Enfolding her, he drew her backward into his arms. "I want you to meet *my lady,*" he said in his quiet, calm way. There was silence. For a moment, Emma lost her anger, the uneasiness, and felt secure.

"Come to the table." The girl who had been so close to Marvin took Marvin and Emma by the hand. Emma suddenly recognized the girl. Kali.

The bright red blouse Kali wore made her dark-tanned skin look almost bronze. Her long hair, now blonde streaked, also had a perm with tensive rings that gave a wild but attractive look. She was taller and thinner than Emma remembered, and she was no longer the demure girl who had held Marvin's hand at vesper.

"I'm so glad Marv brought you along," Kali said to Emma. "This is my last fling before my mother returns from Europe. Stick around."

Emma did not miss the sarcasm. The nerve of Marvin, she thought, bringing me to *her* house, of all places. The anger she had felt returned. As they came closer to the table set with covered, heavy silver serving dishes, Emma noticed a fancy keg with beer on tap. The effects of Kali's affectionate stance with Marvin destroyed Emma's desire for food; however, the table looked inviting. Maybe there were goodies under those covers worth nibbling.

Emma was stunned when she uncovered qualudes, pink hearts, and black beauties—uppers, downers, speed—all for the choosing. Other dishes offered solid, well-rolled joints and small squares of something that looked like dirt; and there was a small crystal dish of what looked like sugar with small spoons. Emma's anger turned to fear and she knew she had no business in that room.

She turned away from the table. The lights, the smells, the eternal music, and now the fear made her feel caged. What if she were caught here? Her mother would die, and her father would kill her.

Marvin sensed something was wrong and followed her immediately.

"Marvin, I'm ready to go," she said.

"The party hasn't started yet, baby. I promised that we're going to learn how to fly. Remember?"

"I'm not sure I can learn. Let's go."

He wrapped her in his arms and let his cheek rest on the top of her head. "Listen, you my woman?"

Emma felt as though she were melting inside. Quickly she moved her head, forcing his cheek off, and looked up into his eyes. "Don't ask me that now. Not here. I'll answer that when we're alone."

"We *are* alone. I'm alone. You're alone. We're alone." He drew her closer. "You're my woman, so you'll stay," he whispered in her ear, "until we're ready to go."

"Feast time, feast time," Kali called as she danced around the room with the crystal bowl and little spoons. Everybody followed her to the center of the room and gathered around as she placed the bowl on the floor.

Marvin took Emma's hand to lead her toward what was becoming a large circle. Emma knew she could not be a part of that. Suddenly she pulled away and ran up the steps.

Marvin followed. "Em, what's wrong?" He grabbed her by the shoulders.

"Nothing's wrong. I just can't."

"What you mean, you can't?" Then he softened, "If you're my woman, you'll learn."

"Oh, please, Marvin. You know I care about you. Why do I have to prove it in that way? Let's go."

"I'm not ready yet. So relax." He held her close and rubbed between her shoulders.

She pulled away. "I don't know your super-rich friends. I'm going home."

"How?"

The thought of having to call her mother almost made her panic. To call her father would be even worse. She remembered the money in her purse and was grateful that her mother always insisted upon it being there. "I'll call a cab," she said.

They waited in the quiet of the upper room. Emma sat on the edge of the white sofa, her feet deep in the soft, velvety-white carpet, trying to cope with her feelings. She loved Marvin. Maybe she shouldn't leave him—but that room below, those people, were just too much for her.

Finally the cab came. Marvin helped her in and instructed the driver to take her home. He pressed the fare into the driver's hand. Emma protested, but Marvin waved them on and the cab pulled away.

All the way home she tried not to think; she tried to drown her thoughts in the beautiful lights, but they no longer charmed her. The questions she did not want to answer surfaced again and again. How could Marvin dare take me to that place? Why did I "flake out" and leave him there? Why couldn't I be at ease and take just one whiff? Just one. What harm could that do? Oh, Marvin, she cried to herself, why couldn't you bring me home? Why did we have to go to that kind of party, which is no party at all?

Her mother was still up. "Emma, you're home early." Her mother was surprised.

"Not that early," Emma said, trying to appear nonchalant.

"It's only five after eleven."

"Then you can get a good night's sleep." Emma did not want to get too close to her mother for fear the odor of that room might be in her clothes, in her hair. So she said, "I had a great time. Good night, Mama."

She lay in her bed, going over every detail of the evening. She felt cheated. Why had she been afraid? Suddenly in her mind's eye flashed the words: *Emma*

Walsh arrested in dope raid. "Oh, my God," she said aloud. And all the fear she had tried to contain overwhelmed her. She knew that she wanted to see Marvin again, but she was relieved to be home in her bed.

Seven

Emma awoke early the next morning remembering the relief she had known just before falling asleep. Now, as she thought of last night and of Marvin, the anger and hurt returned.

Had her mother gone through that with Jody— being at the same parties, at the same places? Of course not! Marvin's not my husband . . . he's a free agent. But he's as much mine as he is Kali's. But what did Kali mean: Marvin can find his way there in his sleep. Is she in that house all by herself? But he took me! She thought of Marvin in Kali's embrace. If only I could be that way, adoring Marvin in front of people like that. Again she could see Kali's arms around Marvin; she knew the anger and shame she felt then was similar to the anger she felt when she first saw her father and Jody embracing. Could what happened to her mother be happening to her?

Suddenly she threw off the cover, got out of bed, and bounded around the room. "Forget Marvin," she said as she started putting things in order.

She pulled shoes from under the bed, hung up clothes that had been strewn around all week. She knew she had to keep busy or she would break down and cry. She restacked records, organized her tapes, threw away old papers, made her desk neat, and put all of her magazines orderly in the rack her mother had insisted she use.

Then she changed her linen, made her bed, and finally was ready to vacuum. She didn't want to wake her mother so she took a minute to survey her results. She had forgotten how the soft yellow walls and the yellow print curtains at her windows gave such a warm feeling. The white desk and built in shelves that held her record player, typewriter, books, and other odds and ends had emerged from all the clutter to give her comfort and courage to adjust posters that had been thrown up haphazardly. She decided to keep Michael Jackson; to take down Teddy Pendergrass and put Stevie Wonder in his place. Wouldn't her mother be pleasantly surprised?

She sat on the side of her bed feeling good about herself, wishing she had some way to make Marvin feel that she was special, too. The debutante ball would do just that. He would certainly take her.

They would have all of that evening and an early morning breakfast. But what if the Golden Slippers refused her? They can't, she reassured herself.

She heard the gospel music from her mother's room and knew that the Sunday morning ritual had begun. She and her mother seldom went to church, but every Sunday they spent part of the day listening to gospel music or to a religious program on TV. Now her mother's favorite song was trumpeting through the house:

Lord, you don't have to move my mountains.
Just give me the strength to climb.
And, Lord, don't take away my stumbling block,
But lead me all around.

The music reinforced her feelings of self-doubt, and she went into her mother's room. Her mother was still in bed with magazines strewn about her.

"Come on in," her mother said, patting the bed for Emma to join her.

"I'm not so clean, Mama! Let me wash up."

"Oh, come on. You're all right."

Emma, pleased that she was accepted as she was, lay on the bed and looked at the *Vogue Pattern* book her mother was holding in her hand.

"These are some of the dresses chosen for the debs," her mother said. "We'll have to decide which you like best so it can be made."

"You really think they're gonna choose me, Ma?"

"One 'no' vote can keep you out. But it looks good in spite of that transfer. We're still working on it."

"Now I really want to do it."

"That transfer is the only thing that has me concerned. But I think we can beat that."

The dresses varied in styles to suit slim or plump girls. Emma, a tall, perfect eight, had difficulty choosing. She could wear any of the styles.

"They are all pretty. I'll have to think about it, but right now I could go for the soft flowing one that has the trainlike effect attached at the shoulder; or the one with the hooped skirt and that pretty lace."

"I like the hooped skirt, too," her mother said. "You'd look lovely in that. Sometimes I'm so proud of you, and then," she looked at Emma and grinned, "I think you're hopeless."

"Aw, Mama."

"But most of the time you're a pretty good girl. Look in my closet. There's a box on the floor. For you."

Emma's hands trembled as she ripped the tape off the box. She rummaged through the tissue and brought out a long, soft, cotton-knit nightshirt in her favorite shrimp pink. "Oh, Mama," she cried, "just what I needed for Dee's slumber party."

"I thought you'd like that. The minute I picked it, I could just see you in it, with the fragile gold chain and gold slipper that come with the deb invitation."

Emma reached over and gave her mother a hug and kiss. With all the problems, she still had the best mother in the world. "You deserve breakfast in bed, and I'm gonna make it." She moved out of the room to the rhythm of:

Oh, happy day, oh, happy day
When Jesus washed my sins away.

Just as she finished preparing the tray to take to her mother's room, the doorbell rang. Who could that be? Her first thought was that it was a member of the Golden Slippers bringing news that she had been accepted.

The tradition was that members of the club notified each girl, individually, at the girl's home, at a chosen hour. All girls would get the word simultaneously, timed to the minute. The suspense was almost unbearable, so that, during the second week of November, every potential deb's heart stopped at the ring of her doorbell.

"I'll get it," she called. Hurriedly she delivered the tray and rushed to the door. It was Marvin.

Oh, no. She was not ready for Marvin, not that early in the morning. Now she wished she had not listened to her mother and had had her shower. She had to let him in.

With the door cracked, she showed only her head. "Hi, give me a minute to run to my room, then you come in and make yourself comfortable while I get presentable, OK?

"It's Marvin, Mama," she said on the way to her room.

When she returned to the living room in a warmup suit, he was sitting, beating out the rhythm of the gospel music on his thigh.

"Well, I doubt that you look any better," he said. "I'd prefer seeing you as you look when you're ready for bed. Or, maybe in nothing." He laughed.

"Aw, Marvin." She lowered her head, embarrassed as always when he teased her in that way. "What are you doing over here so early?"

"I came to see if you got home all right."

"Little you care. If you cared, you wouldn't have taken me there in the first place. Right?"

"Wrong. Because I care, baby, I want you to know everything about me. And I want to know everything about you."

"There are some things I'd rather *not* know. Kali is one of them. I'm not the kind to love my rivals. Nor am I the kind to let you burn me and pretend it doesn't hurt."

"She's no rival."

"Well, she was putting down some heavy stuff— 'You can find your way in your sleep.' I was listening, all right."

"Were you listening when I introduced you as *my lady*?"

Emma said nothing.

"I'm talking to you, woman. Were you listening?"

"That doesn't mean a thing. You let me come home in a taxi! Wait just a minute and I'll give you back the fare." She rushed off to her room and returned with five dollars.

"No, thanks. My old man always told me if I took a lady out, I must see that she gets home, safe."

"I'm sure your father didn't mean putting a girl in a taxi. Were you concerned about what your father said, or were you more interested in what was going down at the party?"

"Listen, Em."

"Don't raise your voice. I don't want Mama to hear us."

"No, you listen," he said quietly. "I asked you, 'How're you gonna get home?' And what did you say? *You* said, 'I'll call a cab.' That was your decision and I took care of it."

"What else could I have done?"

"You could have said, *'You're taking me.'* I'd have had no other choice and I would have brought you home."

"You think I believe that?" she said with controlled rage. "You can make a better case of messing up than anybody I know."

"I'm not the son of a good lawyer for nothing." He laughed. "You're something else when you lose your cool, you know that?" He took her hands and tried to bring her into his arms.

"No way." She pushed him in the chest away from her. "I'm mad at you."

"Emma," her mother called from her room. "Did you offer Marvin some breakfast?"

"He doesn't want any."

"Yes, I do, Mrs. Walsh."

"Fix Marvin some breakfast," her mother said.

Later, when she walked Marvin to the door, he said, "Thanks for a pleasant morning, and for a good breakfast. I'm looking forward to spending an evening with you and taking you to breakfast, soon."

"I'm looking forward to that, too."

He held her hands. "You glad I came?"

She nodded her head yes. She was glad that she had spent that time with him. But deep down under she knew something was missing. Suddenly she remembered her mother's words: *"Don't let yourself become accustomed to being grateful for nothing."*

Eight

The week of waiting for the announcement of the chosen debs and the anticipation of the slumber party were just too much. To help reduce the tension, Emma spent most of her time alone in the library, studying or reading. She ignored Brenda and her crowd and gave them lots of space.

Finally, the waiting was almost over and that Friday afternoon Emma rushed out of class to the curb where her mother waited. All that week she had gone home expecting the doorbell to ring. Hours were spent on the telephone with Dee or Cheryl, talking, planning, or dreaming. Now they would spend the night talking, planning, and dreaming.

Emma sat looking out of the car window, too

excited to talk. What if the announcement came while she was at Dee's? What if she were not accepted and the others were? What would she do at that party with them all knowing? Oh, if Ms. Simmons had never existed. But she was not going to think about that. She was going to that party and have a good time.

At home she went to her room and checked her overnight bag and her makeup kit; everything was in place. She had folded her nightie and a change of clothes in tissue, her hair rollers, nail polish, a new kind of makeup, all were there. She knew she should take a nap so that she would be the last to succumb to sleep, but she was too excited. She paced back and forth around the room wishing she had the desire to pick up things that had accumulated over the week to clutter the place again.

Finally, she stood looking out her window. Girls from the parochial school in their uniform—pleated skirt, short jacket, blouse with round collar and ribbon tie—walked by. How can they put on that outfit everyday, looking like everyone else? Emma wondered as she watched them. The plump one plodded along while the other, who was tiny for a high school student, walked as if she were trying to restrain an urge to move faster. What were they talking about? Not clothes, not makeup. Boys? . . . Probably. Problems with other girls, more likely.

Two boys followed, completely unaware of the girls, practicing soccer techniques. One walked backward as gracefully as a ballet dancer, bouncing the ball off his head, off his knee, off his toes, to the guy in front of him. The other guy tried mimicking the technique, but failed miserably. Emma laughed when, in frustration, the awkward one hit the ball with both hands. They moved on toward their houses as the twilight changed to darkness.

Emma lay on her bed and listened to sounds of early evening—people rushing home in their cars, the hum of motors and the swish of tires coming in waves like the sound of wind in trees, or the roll of the sea. She got off her bed and looked into the mirror. She lifted her hair onto the top of her head, turned on a cool stare, her nose turned upward. Then she asked herself, Why would a smart girl like you want to be a debutante?

"Emma," her mother called. "Are you ready?"

"Is it that time? So soon?" Suddenly she felt a compelling urge to stay home. The old fear of being rejected by the Golden Slippers haunted her again, and she sighed. She *would* be accepted. She must hold on to that thought and nothing else.

When her mother dropped her off at Dee's house, Emma asked, "What if it comes tonight?"

"I'll call you."

"Even if it's late?"

"Never too late for good news. Don't worry now. Have a good time."

As Emma struggled up to the door with her kit, overnight case, and sleeping bag, the noise came from the kitchen, which was near the front of Dee's house. Everyone was there: Linda, Cheryl, Tanya, Melanie, and Diane. After Emma was greeted with squeals of welcome, Dee's mother relieved her of the sleeping bag and guided her upstairs to the recreation room to deposit her things. The room was filled with all the necessary equipment to make a slumber party a success.

Emma was just in time for dinner. Noise faded as the food was sampled. "Dee, you intend to fatten us with pizza, spaghetti, desserts, and all this stuff," Emma said as she filled her plate.

"Don't you just love it?" Tanya said.

"I love it, but can't afford it," Linda said. "I've gotta lose ten pounds before the ball."

"You don't have much time," Cheryl said.

The conversation quickly shifted to the dress patterns that had been chosen. Tanya and Melanie had selected the chiffon pattern that was also one of Emma's choices.

Immediately after dinner they rushed upstairs and exchanged makeup. They did each other's fingernails and toenails in black, silver, and frosted shades. Each girl's head bustled with hair rollers.

They all agreed that Emma's nightshirt was really fit for the ball, and that the color did wonders for her lovely brown skin. As the evening wore on, Emma lost all sense of doubt and uneasiness. She joined in all the fun.

With the music just low enough to keep Dee's

mother from complaining, they learned the latest steps from Tanya, who was the best dancer in the group.

"Can't you see us dancing a cotillion in this day and age?" Tanya referred to the dance they would have to do after their introduction at the ball.

"My boyfriend threatened not to go because he feels he can't learn that cold, stiff dance. Why not the gigolo?" Diane said and they all cracked up.

"Why not? Anything but a cotillion," Dee said, trying to mimic Tanya doing the robot.

Exhausted, they settled in their sleeping bags. Melanie, who had been quiet all evening, fumbled in her bag and brought out a silver flask.

"My mother won't like that, Melanie," Dee said.

"She doesn't have to know," Melanie said. "Anybody? It's bourbon, the best."

Emma looked at Dee, who was trying to contain her anger. That drinking was the reason why Dee had not wanted Melanie at the party. Melanie could not do without booze no matter what the occasion, and Dee's mother was strict when it came to drugs and alcohol. However, Melanie was there because Dee's mother had insisted.

Only Diane accepted. Melanie then took a long drink and put the flask away.

"Why were you late, Em?" Melanie asked, breaking the silence.

"I wasn't late."

"We thought you might not come," Melanie said.

"Why would you think that?" Emma asked.

" 'Cause, we wanted you to come so badly. We miss you, girl," Linda called out.

"Yeah, things ain't what they used to be at Marlborough since you left," Cheryl said.

"We don't know what's going down. The crackers are in complete control." Everybody laughed at Dee's words.

"They always were," Emma stated matter-of-factly.

"No, now, Em. At least you were our representative. We have nobody now," Diane said.

"And, girl, the white chicks are just taking Marvin over." Melanie's voice had a tinge of anger.

"And who else?" Emma asked. She didn't want the conversation centered around Marvin and his women. Did they know about Kali? She hoped not.

"Anybody they think have potential. It's disgusting." Quiet Melanie was letting her anger show.

Emma said nothing, hoping the conversation would die. She didn't want to get into that black-man-white-woman thing.

"Maybe they think they're doing us a favor," Cheryl said. Emma then knew that the topic would have to run its course.

"A favor?" they all cried.

"If that's a favor, heaven help us if they ever decide to do us in." Dee shrugged and sighed deeply.

"Dee?" Cheryl asked. "You remember that book

we read about the white chick who took a Black dude from a sister? Emma, you read it, too."

Emma remembered having read the book and how it had angered and hurt her. She didn't want to talk about it.

"This chick in the book thought she was doing Blacks a favor. And, of course, you know what kind of dude he was," Cheryl said.

"Had to be good looking," Linda blurted out.

"A great basketball, football, and soccer player rolled in one," Melanie added.

"And a brain, etcetera, etcetera, etcetera," Diane said.

"Wait, wait," Dee shouted. "This dude was all that, *plus* he was a *black* Black with blue eyes, yet." They all cracked up.

"You guys making that up," Tanya said.

"Un-unh!" Dee cried. "And don't laugh, this is serious. The chick who took the dude said she did it because we didn't know how to be feminine and how to treat our men: We go out and get all the jobs, take care of the family, and make our men lean on us. *Our men* need somebody to lean on them so that they can prove their manhood."

Emma remembered how confused she had been when she read that part of the book. She had wondered at that time if her mother was to blame for her father marrying Jody. But since then she had learned to ask other questions. Had her mother not worked then to help her father, would Jody be able to lean on him now? She wished they would talk about something else.

"I thought you lean on your father," Diane said. "I want to be a partner, working together on equal footing with my husband. I ain't looking for no father in my man. But what I want to know is, what did the sister do, Cheryl?"

"The sister freaked out—quit a library job to wait tables—"

"Worse than that, she *quit school* over that dude," Dee interrupted.

"And some other sisters did a stupid thing, too. They cut off the chick's hair," Cheryl continued.

"Sounds like that writer put us down," Melanie said. "They wouldn't cut *hair*. Hair will grow back. They would've branded her for good." There was a burst of laughter.

The laughing was contagious so Emma laughed, too; but she was thinking about Kali and Marvin, Jody and her mother, Manning and Marlborough. She knew she was caught in a whirl of color that never ceased. She wanted to do something to stop the talk, but she didn't know what to do. She was the only one there whose father was married to a white woman; and it was Marvin who was being vamped by white girls, so what could she say? She wanted to ask: What choice do we have? Do we Black women do what we do because we want to, or because we have to? She thought of the old saying "You can't lean on a broken stick." Seems like to me we're being asked to take the blame for not leaning on a *stick that was broken by the people doing the blaming,* but she said nothing.

In the middle of the laughter, the doorbell rang. It was as though lightning had struck. The laughing ceased. Nobody moved, yet the anticipation in the room seemed to crackle in the silence.

"Dee. Dee, come down here," Dee's mother called.

They all scrambled up and, as one, they tumbled down the stairs. A member of the Golden Slippers Club stood near the door with a gold envelope in her hand. "Dedrie, congratulations! You have been chosen as a Golden Slipper's debutante for this year. We are proud to honor you." The statement was friendly, but formally made.

Everybody stood breathless, waiting as Dee nervously broke the heavy seal and brought forth the gold invitation for her and an escort to attend the ball. Then the gold chain with the golden slipper was placed around Dee's neck. Squeals shattered the silence as the girls hugged and kissed Dee in joy.

The telephone started ringing. Other visitations had been made. Each time the phone rang Emma's heart stopped, then pounded wildly until someone had been called. Laughter and tears of relief flowed as each congratulated the other.

Why didn't her mother call? Emma wondered whenever the phone was silent for a minute. Then there were only two girls left. The phone rang. Emma was not called. She waited and waited.

"Call home," Dee suggested. "Your mother couldn't get through. The line has been busy. Call, Em."

"It's no use. I'll not make a debut this year," she said, trying to appear lighthearted; but her heart was like lead and her mouth was dry, her eyes burning with unshed tears.

The joy the others felt could not be subdued and Emma remembered words she had read somewhere: "Those who look upon the dead have a sudden rush of joy because they are alive." She knew that each girl mourned for her, but was also delighted it was not she who had been rejected. She understood and was happy for them all.

She lay in her sleeping bag wondering, Why me? How could they have rejected her? If only she could move back the time. Oh, God, she prayed, why do this to me? Will I go on forever paying for one stupid mistake? She felt as though she would crumble inside. She must not let go. A sound alerted her. Then she saw Melanie's flask in the darkness and she wanted to call out. Maybe she should share that flask and forget it all; but she felt that if she moved and said a word, she would shatter into a thousand pieces. She lay there hanging on.

Then the phone was ringing, ringing, ringing. She was running to answer it, but she couldn't find it. Where was it? She ran through every room hoping it would not stop ringing before she got to it. Suddenly she knew that someone was hiding the phone from her. She began to cry. It's only a game of hide-and-seek. *Stop that crying!* I don't want to play a game, she screamed. The phone stopped ringing; the shock of the silence woke her.

She shot up. Her sleeping bag was wet with tears. The girls around her were breathing evenly, dead in slumber. She made her way, quietly, through the sleeping girls, down the stairs. In the back of the house, near the sliding door of Dee's living room, she looked out at the blue water of the swimming pool. Day was dawning and the lights reflecting in the water were losing their power to the light of day.

Silent tears streamed down her face as she wondered, Could it be true that there are people in the world who do not wish me well? And then she thought, No, my invitation is there, at home. Mama wants to surprise me. A sob escaped her throat. She knew better. Suddenly she realized she could not face those girls. She found the telephone. "Mama, I want to come home. Yes. Now, please, come."

Nine

By the time her mother got her home, Emma felt she had cried herself dry, but she shook as if she had been seized by a fit of shivering. Her mother helped her through a warm bath, insisting all the while on trying to soothe her with the thought that it was a mistake. She would straighten it out.

Finally, in bed with a hot water bottle at her feet, Emma sipped warm milk. Her mother sat on her bed in silence until the milk was finished, then left the room. Emma slept fitfully, her sleep disturbed with unpleasant dreams that woke her frequently. One that she forgot immediately upon waking left her frightened.

She sat up in bed and realized it was one o'clock

in the afternoon. The quiet in the house drove her from her bed in search of her mother. In the hallway, voices filtered through to her from the kitchen.

"You know, you sound as if you're happy that she's rejected," her mother said. "What's with you, Larry? Are you ashamed of Emma, or is it that you don't expect much from her?"

"Don't go putting what you feel off on me. I'm merely being realistic. Blacks who have *class* are no different from any other people with class—thank God for that—and anybody wanting to be considered by those with class have to measure up," her father said.

"And you think your daughter doesn't measure up because she was railroaded out of Marlborough?"

Emma became rigid at the asking of that question. Did her mother really feel that Ms. Simmons had lied and had never admitted it before? She wanted to rush in and interrupt the conversation, but she didn't want them to know she was eavesdropping. She turned to go to her room, but stopped when her father answered, "Let's not be dishonest. Emma was not without guilt. We had both noticed the chip on her shoulder. . . ."

"Is that reason enough to be transferred? I made the mistake to let them force me to confront them without Emma. I never had their word and Emma's at the same time. And, of course, you were no help at all. I'm just tired of fighting battles alone."

"Isn't it possible she cursed? Here lately she's been

acting like a lot of Blacks who think all authority is racist."

How could he take the side of Ms. Simmons? Emma thought as her anger flared.

"I can remember in the sixties when you were afire with Blackness and *knew* most authority *is* racist, and I know who cooled your fire; but that is not the issue. The real issue is: We didn't go to bat for Emma and left her out on a limb. If I had thought for one moment our so-called friends would cut her off, I'd never given in that easily." Her mother's anger showed.

"Why are you so surprised, Janet? Has there been a Manning girl a Golden Slipper debutante, ever?"

"Emma is not 'a Manning girl,' and you know it."

"She's there. Let's face it."

"Listen, Larry, those people are *your* friends, more so than mine. Will you talk to them? Rules can be broken."

"I don't know what good it will do. Whether Emma is a good girl, or bad, Manning girls are not considered Golden Slipper material. That's that."

"Are you saying you won't ask? I think it's just a mistake."

"I'm not saying I will and I'm not saying I won't; I'm just stating a fact."

"Larry, we don't ask much of you. I don't ask anything for myself, but I'm begging you now. Do this for Emma."

Emma heard the tears in her mother's voice, and

forgetting she was eavesdropping, rushed into the kitchen and put her arms around her mother. "Mama, don't beg him. I don't want it. If they offer it now, I won't take it."

She looked at her father, who sat at the table eating an apple, looking boyish in an English wool sweater and cords. There was something about him that reminded her of Marvin. With others he was warm, friendly, even playful. She wished he was that way with her. Now he sat with his eyes down, refusing to look at her.

The look on her mother's face made her know she had done an awful thing to interfere.

"You can't make that decision," her mother shouted as Emma fled the room.

Her mother followed and found Emma staring out her window. "Emma, you don't know what you're saying. I want you to calm yourself and think this through."

"I am calm."

"Come here and sit down," her mother demanded. Her mother sat on the rumpled bed. Emma sat, tailor-fashion, on the floor. "You have worked too hard for this and you deserve it as much as any girl chosen, more than some."

The fight has come too late with the wrong people, Emma thought. Why had her mother let Ms. Simmons off the hook so easily? Why hadn't she insisted on bringing that incident into the open? Emma said nothing.

"You can't see it now, Emma, but these activities are important. They are necessary if you want to be a part of things. Later, you might want to join a sorority or a nice social club. Having been a deb will help, Emma. It opens doors. You understand?"

"Mama, I . . . I thought it would be fun. And I like most of those girls, but . . . can't you understand? What would it look like being there when they all know I was not accepted—until Daddy put the pressure on."

"It's not 'putting pressure on,' " her mother said, mimicking Emma. "It's letting them know they cannot cast you aside as if you're a . . . a nobody."

"Call it what you will, Mama. I can't. Not with my friends."

"Now you listen to me. I'm going to call your father in here, and you're going to tell him that you *want* this, and *you're going to have it.*"

Emma looked around her room: clothes about, bed unmade. She felt trapped. "Oh, no, he can't come in here." She felt ashamed and angry that she had to face her father; and, now, mixed with that anger was the anguish from feeling that her father was ashamed of her.

"I'm going to call him," her mother said.

"No. Please, wait. I'll go out there and talk to him."

Her father was still at the table. He did not look at Emma as she moved into the room and stood, her back against the refrigerator.

"Emma has something to say to you," her mother said, standing near the table where Emma's father sat.

Emma was taken off guard by that direct approach. Suddenly she realized that she could not say what her mother wanted said. She kept her eyes down, feeling the angry humiliation she had felt when she heard her mother begging.

"So? Did she change her mind? Should we pursue this further?" her father asked.

"Isn't it too late?" Emma asked. She wanted to scream at her father, Why did you let me go to Manning if you knew?

"No, it's not too late. She wants it," her mother said.

"I'll do my best," her father said.

Emma went to her room, wondering why her mother kept insisting that it was a mistake. But maybe she should be thankful for their efforts. Then she remembered the humiliation, shame, and hurt when her friends had been accepted. How could she face them, even if her father reversed the decision?

She must have fallen asleep again, for when she was startled by a knock on her door the streetlamp was on. Her mother was calling.

"What day is it?" Emma asked, scrambling out of bed.

"It's Saturday, and Marvin is here."

She looked in the mirror. Her eyes were swollen, her face drawn; she was a mess. "Tell him to wait," she cried and rushed to bathe her face in cold water, trying to restore some of its moisture. She decided against any makeup.

Her mother and Marvin were enjoying a good laugh at something. They had an easy way with each other, but when Emma entered the room, her mother left them alone.

"Hi, Marvin." Emma moved toward him, fighting the urge to cry. "I'm so glad you've come. I had hoped you'd call."

"I did call. Your mother asked me to come over." He held her close.

"Oh," Emma said, drawing away from his embrace. She sat on the sofa.

"I heard the bids were out, so I called to congratulate you. Your mother told me the news." He sat beside her, but on the edge of the sofa facing her.

The hurt returned. She had wanted this so much for them. To spend that time with him. Now that chance was gone. Maybe her father would succeed; and for a moment she didn't dare think of the consequences, she only hoped.

As if knowing her thoughts, Marvin said, "There's still a chance."

She thought of the humiliation and said, "I think I'm crazy to hope. I should admit it: It's not really what I want."

"What do you mean, not what you want?"

"Marvin, you don't understand. . . ."

"I understand. This is *the* social event of the year.

Everybody—*who is anybody*—will be there. And you say it's not what you want?"

She struggled to fight back the tears. She must not let him think that she was being insensitive. "Well . . . it's not as simple as my not wanting it. . . ."

"It is as simple as: A mistake was made and corrected. All you have to do is pull it off with class, Em."

Emma laughed.

"Why you laughing? All you have to do is act as though the mistake never occurred and get on with it, have a ball."

"I can't do that."

"How can you *not* do it? How can you hurt your mother? And how can you do that to us?"

"I don't see what it has to do with us."

"To *me,* then?"

The hurt and sorrow she had felt about not being able to go flared into anger. How could he even think she could refuse to go just to hurt him? Then maybe she was being selfish. But suppose the decision was not reversed. She couldn't keep vacillating back and forth with all the hurt and humiliation. "I'm sorry if you think I'm being mean. I'm not. I thought you, of all people, would understand."

"Listen, baby, you know I had looked forward to going to that ball with you. I wanted it and I thought you did, too."

"I did, Marvin."

"Well, I intend to go with or without you. I'd

much rather be going with you. You can understand that, can't you?"

She couldn't believe what he was saying, nor did she understand the mixture of hurt and anger dissolving so quickly when he took both of her hands. She suddenly knew she didn't want to lose him, yet she knew she did not want to face her friends in humiliation again. She could hardly hold back the tears. She did not look at him when she whispered, "Yes, I understand."

He then held her face, pressuring her to look up into his eyes. She glanced at the long slender fingers of his strong hands and felt a rush of love; but she turned aside quickly and said, "Please, Marvin, go."

Before she had time to recover from Marvin's departure, the phone rang. Her mother reached the phone first. Emma stood close by. The look on her mother's face told the story. "It's your father. It has nothing to do with you, Emma, they said. It's the rules. If they let you, then they would have to deal with applications from other Manning girls, and . . . "

Emma did not wait to hear more. Her nightmare was over. Or was it beginning, with the season to be jolly just ahead?

Ten

The past weekend had been so unsettling that neither Emma nor her mother could spring back easily into the regular routine. Emma got to Manning late Monday morning. The crowd had already gathered; and with only three days of school before Thanksgiving and winter vacation only three weeks away, a festive holiday mood had taken over. Even Emma felt charged.

She sensed the powerful exhilaration that could often move quickly to uncertainty and even apprehension. There was nothing like this atmosphere at Marlborough. A burst of laughter here, boisterous shouts there, jest and humor everywhere that might spark laughter, or an angry response that could explode into a violent scene, but often was easily smothered in more joking.

She hurried by three white teachers standing together. One, Mr. Kooner, had his hands in his pockets, shoulders drawn up, eyes alert. He looked very ordinary, but was doing his best to appear in control. He was not talking with the others, yet seemed bound together with them in that sea of energy. What was he thinking?

She remembered how alone she often felt at Marlborough. But it was not exactly loneliness. How could she put it? Intimidated. Not knowing what to expect, trying to hold on until she was with those few Blacks, relieved to be herself again. Was Mr. Kooner intimidated?

"Whew!" she exclaimed, mopping faked perspiration from her brow when she finally reached Allan, who was waiting in the usual place. "I didn't think I'd make it. Boy, this crowd! It's exciting, but, you know, it's a little scary, too. All that energy. Something's here that I just can't explain."

The bell rang. "Oh, no," Emma cried. "I gotta talk to you, Allan." The frustration and hurt needed release through talk.

"All that hassle with you last week, I gotta know what's up with the ball. Did the bid come?" Allan asked as they walked toward their classes.

"Stay for fifth period today," Emma pleaded.

"You know I can't stick around here for lunch."

"Listen, I packed some food for us. Stay and we'll talk." Emma started into her classroom.

"Tell me, just tell me. Did it come?" Allan shouted after her.

"Tell me, just tell me," Emma repeated to herself and smiled as she waited for Allan to join her on the steps at lunchtime. She was glad she had remembered the night before to make tuna sandwiches, for she barely had time that morning to grab apples and brownies to stuff into the lunch bag.

The noon crowd was thickening. By now Emma was beginning to place names on many faces. But who would not remember Carrie, the climber. Carrie, Emma thought, might be fun to know, but how could anybody outside get close to Carrie? Walt, her boyfriend and constant companion, had not yet arrived, but Carrie's usual entourage of fellows was there.

James, a favorite football player and boojei, had cornered the fountain for his crowd; and the little group of elitist scientists who monitored Eoil Can and his feathered friends were already in place. Emma wondered what had happened to Brenda. She hadn't been around all day. Brenda was often absent, leaving her not-too-cohesive group like a body without a head. What's keeping Allan? she asked herself.

Emma watched people show passes coming in and out of a nearby exit and realized that nothing like that existed at Marlborough either. There, students came and went as they pleased on their own. Suddenly she was aware that students without passes could not get in. They were not only locked in at this place; at a certain time of day, without a pass, they were locked out.

At this exit, students without passes were trying to get out. They were having little luck. Every gate without a guard was locked. One boy tried bribery, then sweet-talking the female guard. Finally he tried threats. Emma had to laugh when he kissed the guard's hand, smiled broadly, and vanished on campus.

Had Allan forgotten? Why didn't he come? Emma took a bite of apple to encourage her appetite. She had not eaten well all weekend.

At last Allan appeared, his tall, lean body in a loosely fitting, worn, olive-drab jacket and pants with many pockets. The baggy pants fitted only around his ankles. His relaxed manner, his smile, and the way he used his hands while talking made him attractive. He appeared aloof, but was really warm and attentive, had a way of listening as though the person talking absorbed all of his thought. Emma was glad he was her friend and pleased at his loyalty. She could depend on Allan.

Suddenly she thought about Marvin, and her heart sank. How could she tell Allan what had happened? But she needed to talk about her rejection. She knew she could not tell him that Marvin had not come through in the crisis. But he would. Marvin loves me, she told herself. She would give him time.

"I just hope the lunch you offering is worth staying here for," Allan said as he plopped down beside her.

Emma divided the sandwiches and gave Allan an apple. "I bet if you were free to come and go as you pleased, staying here wouldn't seem bad at all. Allan, how could you choose this school, anyway?"

"First things first." He bit into a sandwich. "Did the bid come?"

"They're out. But I didn't get one." Emma was surprised at the ease in which she said those words. No choking up.

"Don't kid around, woman."

"I'm not kidding."

"What happened?"

"It seems as if Manning is not as well thought of in some circles as it is by you."

"Manning is fine if you don't want things like being a debutante with the Golden Slippers. Why did you come here?"

"I didn't *choose* to come. I lost my cool." She felt an uncontrollable anger. "And if I could damn that teacher to hell's fire now, I'd feel much better."

"Teacher trouble, eh?"

"Yeah, a Ms. Simmons. Oh, Allan, she pretended to like me so much. And maybe she did, in her way.

I know I didn't *dislike* her. She always seemed amazed, surprised that I'm me. So she chose me as her thing. She was really about undoing me so she could do me up the way she wanted me to be. Always pushing, pushing, pushing. She and the girl's V.P., always making me out to be different from other Blacks. It finally got to me and I ended up here."

"Then you get here and find this school is no place to be part of the upper crust even when you are the upper crust."

"Why? Why are girls from here not debs?"

"Maybe the girls here don't ask to be."

"You don't ask, Allan, you're chosen."

"Maybe for the same reasons that Golden Slipper debs aren't Rose Bowl queens." Allan laughed.

"Aw, Allan, stop clowning."

"Looks like the same reason to me—Manning girls are different from Golden Slippers girls. . . ."

"And Golden Slippers girls are different from Rose Bowl queens." Emma mimicked him, exasperated. "I just think it's stupid. There are some nice girls here."

"Nice, good, bad has nothing to do with it. If it did, then the rules could be flexible, for those terms are relative, Emma."

"I guess it's as my father said. 'If you want to be considered by people with class, you have to measure up.' "

"Yes, you have to be *just like them.*"

"This is a crazy world. I'm really confused. Come

on, Allan, tell me. You're a smart dude, well read, a National Honor student. You could have chosen any school in the city—and you come here. Why? I want to know, why?"

"I no longer thought the opportunity transfer an opportunity. I've bused since I was in the second grade and all those years they tried to make me out to be different."

"But you are different."

"So are we all. And we are all alike in certain ways, too. What bothers me is that the ways we are different are always out front there to make some of us feel bad about ourselves and others feel great about themselves. I was always told how different I was from other Blacks. . . ."

"Yeah," Emma said, thinking about Ms. Simmons. "The hall walkers, the riffraff."

"Exactly. But I kept seeing how different I am from whites. They'd tell all kinds of jokes about us, right in front of me; play horrible games; and, yet, you could almost swear they meant to be friendly."

Allan went on to tell Emma about the time when he was in the second grade—the only Black in the class. The teacher had them all record their voices on a tape. When it was Allan's turn, the teacher changed the speed, creating a sound like Donald Duck. "Everybody cracked up," Allan said. "It blew my mind. I didn't know anything about tape recorders and speed change. I thought that was *me*."

Emma laughed. "What did you think when he gave you another chance?"

"He didn't. I was left believing I sounded like that."

"Oh, Allan." Emma felt the hurt, too, as she remembered an incident at Marlborough. "Something similar happened to me in an honors science class. I was the only Black. I gave a report on Dr. Charles Drew."

"The one who first preserved blood plasma and organized the first blood bank."

"Yeah. When I finished my report, a boy in the class, real smart—nicknamed Eieny—for you know who. Anyway, he said, 'If this Dr. Drew had done something like that, especially during World War II with all those wounded people, his name would be a household word. Who in here ever heard of him? Who? Nobody.' Then he asked the teacher, 'You ever heard of this Dr. Drew?' Allan, that teacher gave me this look and called for the next report. Then everybody looked at me as if I had made all of that up."

"Did the teacher ever bring it up again after he did his homework?"

"Not while I was in there." They were silent. Finally Emma said, "Is that why you came back to Manning?"

"It's not that simple. Out there I was chosen. Here I can choose."

"What's wrong with being chosen?" Emma demanded. "I wanted to be chosen by the Golden Slippers."

"And you were turned down, too." He saw the hurt look in her face and quickly said, "To want to be chosen is all right. But I've learned that inherent in being chosen is that possibility of being rejected for reasons you can't do anything about. You're at the mercy of the choice makers. They usually want you to do things that mean the most to them, not to you. I like science, love music, I'm good in math, but they were trying to jam me into accounting."

Was Allan trying to tell her that those things so hard to verify, which had caused so much frustration at Marlborough, were actually designed to limit her and her friends? Suddenly she realized that though she was never actually denied membership in the Science Club, she was unable to find out the requirements and never knew when and where meetings were held. When she inquired about the Foreign Language Club, she was urged to join the well-integrated Glee Club. How had Allan become so aware? she wondered.

"Now here at Manning," Allan continued, "I can be a part of almost anything that exists; and if I want something that doesn't exist, I can put things in motion to make it happen."

"You believe that, Allan?"

"Well, the possibility, yes. And, too, those people out there were not a real part of my life. Out of the people here will come some of my lifelong friends; but beyond all that, Emma, here I can relax and just be myself."

Emma smiled, thinking of how she had felt just that morning—a little scared, but certainly not intimidated the way she had felt at Marlborough. Still, she was not sure. "Are you happy, Allan? Here, I mean."

"Happy? Well, sometimes, yes. Sometimes, no. But I can say I'm more at ease than I am diseased. I was really in a state of disease out there." He laughed. "Get it? *Not myself at all.*"

This is his last year in this place. Where will he go from here? she wondered.

As if he were reading her thoughts, Allan said, "I believe that being out there in elementary and junior high, and back here in high school, will put me in good shape to go to *any* college, especially a mixed one. *I know who I am.*"

Emma wished she were as self-confident as Allan. She was still confused, wishing at times she were back at Marlborough. She thought of Marvin and of her other friends. "You came to your friends, Allan. I left mine. It's not easy here. Seniors are satisfied with their cliques, and there is little time for, and less interest in, newcomers." She fought to keep back the tears.

"It's not *that* bad. Ole Marv will be around, I'm sure."

"Don't bet on it." She suddenly wished she had

not said that. She still didn't want Allan to know Marvin had not come through in the crisis.

"I'll bet on him and your other friends, too." He took her hand in both of his. "You're an OK lady, Em."

"My friends are all right. Say, one of them who saw you at the game was so impressed she wants you to come to a party during the winter break. Her name is Cheryl. She's dying for you to come."

"I accept. So keep her alive until after the party, OK?"

Emma sat letting him hold her hand, thinking about all he had said. The old pain of rejection returned. She couldn't finish her lunch. She handed him her sandwich and brownie.

"The lunch was worth staying for." He looked at her, grinned, and released her hand.

A roar went up from the crowd. The sea gulls winged in on time to feed. Allan protected his sandwich and brownie, but Eoil Can was not in the squad.

"I know the odds are great against it, Emma, but I hope you'll learn to like here."

"With your friendship, I'm sure that even if this coming semester does not *make* me, it certainly will not *break* me; and with your promise to come to the party, I can now look forward to the holiday."

Eleven

The traffic and the rush were terrific, but not unusual for the holiday season. People on the bus were loaded down with packages, folded baby strollers, and large transistors. Old ladies wrapped in furs and fake pearls got on and off slowly. Going where? Emma wondered as she mentally urged the bus driver on. The driver seemed in no hurry, oblivious of her need to make it to her father's office before he left at four o'clock.

It was now a little after three o'clock. Besides the snarled traffic, the driver seemed deliberately to miss every light. In a holiday mood, he flirted with the old ladies, making them blush and bloom.

Emma sat by the window hardly able to keep

from laughing at the driver's banter. Suddenly she thought of Marvin and was again plunged into gloom. How could he have done what he did without letting her know? Could that be why he hadn't called since the winter vacation began? She could hear Dee now: ". . . and Marvin was there."

Dee had come by early that morning, on her way to the hairdresser, to show Emma copies of her pictures that would be included in the souvenir book of the ball. Pictures of all the girls, their escorts, and members of the Golden Slippers would also be included, along with congratulatory remarks from leading professional and business people.

Dee brought Emma up to date. The past weeks had been spent in a whirlwind of social events and business of the ball: picture taking, dress fittings, shopping, rehearsals. There had been receptions, teas, news conferences. Dee went on and on, especially animated over the party Melanie's mother had given for the girls and their escorts. "Marvin was there," she said.

"Marvin? What was Marvin doing there?" Emma demanded.

Dee tried to soften the blow, "Oh, Emma, I thought you knew. Marvin's taking Melanie tonight."

"Melanie?" Emma let out a strange laugh, trying to disguise the deep hurt, but she could not pull it off. "I don't believe that! Marvin wouldn't do such a thing." Surely he would have told her himself. He wouldn't let her hear it through the grapevine. She could forgive Marvin anything but that. Finally, she said, "Well!"

"Exactly what I said when I saw him there. Everybody's mad at him and Melanie. But, you know Melanie. She'll do anything for attention."

"I know *Marvin.*"

"Emma, did you get my invitation to the ball?"

"Yeah. For me and Mama."

"Are you coming?"

"You kidding?"

"Aw, come," Dee pleaded. "I want you there. We all want you."

"Who would I come with?" Emma laughed.

"That's why we're so mad at Marvin. And especially at Melanie. Acting as though Marvin's her steady, when all *he* wants is to be an escort. He knew all the time you'd be an invited guest."

Emma listened, hardly able to control the anger that moved to hurt, to humiliation, to sorrow as Dee continued to pour out news and gossip. Emma feigned enthusiasm, but she was glad when Dee left. She rushed to the phone and angrily dialed Marvin. There was no answer. She suddenly knew she could not stand the pressure. She would go see her father and ask him to, please, let her go away.

Now as she got off the bus to walk the short distance to the office, she was glad Marvin had not answered. Although the ball was that evening, he still had time to let her know he was escorting

Melanie. But would he? She remembered his words: "I intend to go, with, or without, you." Suddenly she had to swallow hard to fight back the tears.

She was just in time. Her father was in the parking lot walking toward his car when she hailed him.

"Well, what a surprise. How'd you get here?"

"On the bus. I'm glad I caught you, Daddy. I need to talk to you." She was pleased that he was apparently glad to see her. She was a bit self-conscious and doubtful. Her heart began to pound as it did when she confronted her father alone. She was not often alone with him these days.

"What's up?" He looked at her and smiled.

She averted her eyes. "I was wondering, Daddy. I need to get away for the holidays, like . . . go someplace else."

"Like where, Emma?"

"Like Hawaii. Mexico."

"Tijuana?" He laughed.

"Oh, no, Daddy. Mazatlán or Mexico City."

"Alone?" he asked, surprised.

Emma suddenly realized she had not thought this through. She had been prompted by anxiety. "Mother would probably go," she said, hoping to retrieve the initiative.

His face tightened. "You've discussed this with your mother?"

Surprised by his displeasure, Emma quickly said, "Oh, no. I thought we could surprise her. It could be a Christmas present from us." She looked at her father and could not understand what she sensed was anger.

"I'll have to talk to your mother about this. Get in, I'll take you home."

She settled in the car, now worried. What would her mother say? Would her mother be able to take off from work for such a trip? She looked at her father, whose jaw was still set, his eyes on the road, his fingers tightly clutching the wheel.

"That's a lot of money," he said, almost as though he were talking to himself.

Emma became angry. Everything she wanted was too much money. "Probably no more than the ball. Maybe not as much," she said, surprised at the tone of her voice.

"What has that to do with it?"

"You promised to take care of that. Why can't we have *that* money?"

"Because I have other plans for *that* money."

Her anger increased. She sat looking straight ahead as he maneuvered through the heavy traffic. Finally she glanced at him. She wanted to ask if he loved her. Why didn't he see she needed his help? She wanted to shout at him, You promised, and that money should be there to get me away from all of this.

As though he were reading her thoughts, her father said, "When you weren't accepted, I made other plans. Your mother—"

"But you promised . . ." she cried and said no

more. Suddenly she realized the car had stopped. She was home. Her father followed her up the walk into the house.

"Emma, is that you?" Her mother came into the hallway, and seeing Emma's father, she said, "I didn't know you were with her, Larry. Can I fix you a drink?"

"No. I want to know why you let Emma think she could go away when I told you I had made some plans when she was no longer considered a deb?" her father asked angrily.

"What are you talking about?"

"I'm talking about Emma demanding the money I promised for her debut so that you and she can go away, that's what. I asked you to arrange for us to exchange gifts early because Jody and I are going away. And now Emma gets this idea. I don't like that kind of double-dealing, Janet."

Emma realized now why her father had become angry. He thought her asking had been prompted by her mother. She was about to speak when her mother spoke up.

"I resent your thinking that I would put Emma up to ask you for anything. I wouldn't expose her to being hurt like that by you."

"What you mean, hurt by me?" her father demanded.

"You listen." Her mother was amazingly calm. "I have never criticized you to Emma behind your back. I have always tried to agree with you when I knew Emma was around. You know why? Because Emma *needs* your love. She needs to love you, you're her father. And I wanted her to think she had your love."

"Are you trying to pretend I don't love Emma?"

"No. These past few days have taught me that Emma has a lot going for her. She has come through this 'putdown' pretty gracefully. So I'm saying to you, that from now on, you're on your own with Emma. Emma can decide whether or not you love her."

Emma was surprised. Was her mother suddenly seeing her as a woman, not as a child anymore?

"And I want you to know, there comes a time, Larry, when the parent becomes the child. *You gonna need Emma's love.* And if you haven't cultivated it, it won't be there for you. Now, I've worked hard today. I'm tired. I haven't even had time to tell Emma that because you will be on the high seas by Christmas, we will exchange gifts with you the day after tomorrow. But I'll get around to that. Right now, all I want you to do is leave my house. Leave me and Emma alone."

Emma saw the look on her father's face and she knew she loved him, wanted to erase the hurt. She started toward him, then looked at her mother. She knew she could not go to him and leave her mother alone, looking devastated, too. She wanted to hold them, bring them together, let them know she needed them both. Her father strode from the room and Emma realized she had forever lost the chance to bring them together again. She rushed to her room and let the tears, pent-up for years, flow. She was crying for her father, her mother, and for Marvin.

Finally, released, she felt relief.

Emma helped her mother prepare for her father's visit, amazed that she had made it through the past two days and nights. The ball was over. Marvin had not called, but she had decorated her tree, wrapped her father's gift, and was now in a good mood, as she anticipated his coming and Cheryl's party later.

Her mother helped arrange the refreshments, then put on her coat. "Emma, wish your father bon voyage and happy holidays. I'll be back in time to take you to Cheryl's party."

"Mama, where you going?" Emma demanded.

"Out."

"You can't. *This is family.* We're always together at Christmas."

"It's not Christmas."

"But you know he won't be here." Why was her mother acting this way all of a sudden? "I thought you love Daddy."

"I do. Because he's your father. Emma, you'll learn there're many kinds of love. You'll also learn that love is an alive thing—like my plants. It needs nurturing, caring for, otherwise it dies. It'll be good for you and your father to be alone and enjoy time together. I hope he brings Jody so that you can get to know her better, too."

When her mother left, Emma arranged and rearranged gifts under the tree. She moved ornaments and replaced them. She was nervous. What would it be like with her father? What if he did bring Jody? She rushed to the kitchen to make sure everything was still in order: homemade bread warming; wine chilling; cheese in place; the cart with glasses; fruitcake and cookies—all homemade.

She answered the doorbell, her heart racing, her hands trembling. Her father was there, alone with presents.

"Come on in."

"No, Jody's waiting in the car."

"Oh, she can come in, too."

"Maybe, just for a minute." He went to the car while Emma waited with the door open. She was glad she had asked them in. She wished she wasn't so nervous.

Now Jody was carrying one of the packages. She smiled and handed the gift to Emma and said, "Merry Christmas, happy holidays . . . whatever."

"Happy holidays, and welcome." Emma placed the gifts under the tree. Jody said no when Emma asked her to take off her coat, but she did accept the invitation to have refreshments.

They sampled all the good things, and before long Jody removed her coat. She was wearing a silk shirt with a matching skirt in multicolored stripes. Jody laughed at the jokes that her husband told about Emma.

"When Emma was a little girl, around four," he said, "she always said she wanted to get married. 'Who're you gonna marry, Emma?' people always asked, and Emma would say, 'My daddy.' " Her father laughed.

"You know better now, don't you, Emma," Jody said.

"Are you suggesting I'm not a good deal for marriage?" her father chuckled good-naturedly.

Emma remembered when she was a little girl and had so much fun with him. She looked at Jody, who was not as tall as she, or her mother, but Jody had long legs, which made her appear taller than she was. Her hair was cut in a shag that, apparently, she did not know how to care for; but she looked happy. She had finally relaxed and was enjoying herself.

When Emma gave them their present, Jody asked if she could open it.

"Feel free. I don't want to open mine though, not yet," Emma said.

They seemed genuinely pleased with the blue-and-white English wool blanket, monogrammed *Jody's Joy*. As they left, Emma wished them bon voyage as her mother had asked her to do. She waved good-bye, pleased that they had stayed so long—a whole hour and a half. The time had gone quickly and it had been nice. Maybe relating to her father, on her own, just might be interesting. He hadn't come through in her crisis, but she was willing to give him time.

Twelve

When people are happy, they look pretty, Emma said to herself as she put on makeup, getting ready for Cheryl's party. She decided she was *not* happy. She would prefer to be going with Marvin, but she knew that she would have to ignore him if he showed. He would show, all right, she was sure of that. Thank goodness Allan would be there. He had called to ask if he could bring a friend who was home from Stanford for the holidays. Could it be a girl? He had better not bring a girl, with all of her friends waiting to look him over. Suppose he brought a white chick? *He wouldn't dare.* Not Allan.

As her mother drove to Cheryl's, Emma told her about her father's visit.

"Did they like my fruitcake?"

"Oh, Mama, they sure did. But I think they liked your bread better. Daddy asked for some to take home. I gave him some cookies, too."

"Good thinking. How're you gonna get home?"

"Call you. Or should I take a taxi?"

"Call me. I don't want you coming alone."

"I'm a big girl, Mama."

"I'll say!" They both laughed.

Emma thought of the possibility of making up with Marvin. "If I get a ride, I'll let you know, OK?" Then she began to worry. How would her friends react to her? Only Dee had come by during the crisis, and only Cheryl had called, just to verify Allan's coming. Would they be glad to see her? She wished Allan had a car so he could have picked her up.

Her mother waited at the curb until Cheryl let her in. The party was underway with mostly girls. Emma was welcomed with squeals of delight. All of the girls who had been at Dee's slumber party were there; girls from Marlborough she hadn't seen since she'd left were there. She looked around, wondering where the fellows were. She hoped the room would not remain full of girls only.

Already Melanie was a frequent visitor to the punch bowl; and Emma learned that Cheryl's idea of two punch bowls was working in Melanie's favor. Cheryl had convinced her mother that a bowl of grapefruit juice would be great for those on a diet, and a heavy, fruity punch would do for the others. Melanie claimed the grapefruit juice for her flask of vodka and was happy.

The music was going and the girls were dancing en masse with those boys who cared to dance. Every time the doorbell rang, Emma's heartbeat quickened. How would she act if Marvin came in?

"Emma, where's Marvin?" Tanya asked.

Emma controlled the impulse to refer the question to Melanie and said, "I haven't heard from him. Ask Cheryl if she invited him."

"Ask me if I invited who?"

"Marvin, Cheryl," Tanya said.

"Yes. But I'm waiting for Emma's Manning friend."

"That's the guest we're all waiting for," Dee shouted.

Fellows dribbled in and out, and soon there were enough for couples to dance. Finally the odor of weed crept through the room. Marvin walked in and Emma's heart flip-flopped. Immediately he was surrounded with admirers. Some welcome for one they were all mad at, she thought.

"The Bacardi for the party is here," Marvin said and produced a bottle of rum for the fruit punch. Everybody cheered and the party took on new life.

Emma waited. She pretended not to notice his watching her, as if he were waiting for her to make the initial move. Finally she went into an adjoining space where Linda was banging on the piano. They formed a duet and played "Chopsticks" against the sound of the record player. Then Emma felt a hand on her shoulder. She looked around. At first she did not recognize the fellow. Suddenly she squealed, "Allan! You're so dressed up."

He hugged her. "I didn't know you played the piano."

"You call that playing? We were just clowning."

"Come, meet my friend and we'll come back to the piano." He pulled her through the crowd, and even before they reached him, Emma knew he was the one. He was older, and he looked so . . . how could she put it? Distinguished. Not the way he was dressed, but the way he stood there: in the crowd, but definitely apart.

"You're Emma," he said. "I would have known you without Allan. He's told me so much about you." He took both of her hands.

"Hey, Gary, did he tell you she belongs to me?" Marvin had interrupted, putting an arm around Emma's shoulder.

"Aw, come off it, man," Gary said, grinning at Marvin. "You can't claim all the beautiful women in the world."

So this was Gary and he knew Marvin. Emma wiggled Marvin's arm off her shoulder. "From Stanford, eh?" She ignored Marvin.

"From the ghetto, attending Stanford."

"All right! Got it. Let's go back to the piano," Emma said, still ignoring Marvin.

"Let me meet some of these fine ladies first," Allan said.

Emma introduced Allan and Gary around the room. There were never enough men at a party. Many of the girls joined them as Allan sat at the piano. Suddenly there was quiet and Emma was surprised as Allan tested the keys. "You didn't tell me you could play," she cried.

He grinned. "You didn't ask me."

The record player was no competition. Everybody wanted Allan to go on playing. Emma danced with Gary again and again. She learned he was a sophomore in pre-med. "So you're going to be a doctor, too," she said.

"Why you say 'too'?"

"My father's a doctor, and I'll be a doctor one of these days."

"So you're not in awe of the profession. Good. I can relax and make some mistakes. Meeting you proves I'm lucky to know Allan."

"Who doesn't feel lucky knowing Allan? He's my ace. How do you know him?"

"We played in a combo together before I left. He's a way-out musician, never had a lesson. But let's not talk about Allan. You're far more interesting. Where will I send my messages to you?"

Suddenly Allan stopped playing. "Start the record player," he said. "I gotta git in one dance, at least." He grabbed Emma.

In the middle of the dance, Marvin moved in.

"What you trying to do, man? You know this is my woman. You guys from the ghetto think you can just come in and take over," he said angrily.

Allan raised both hands and laughed as if to say he was not armed. "Say, man, I don't intend to take over. She's your lady. I understand that." Allan moved away.

"No, Allan," Emma said, taking his hand. "Let's finish this dance."

"You come over here with me," Marvin demanded, taking Emma by the arm.

To avoid a scene, Emma followed him into a corner. "Listen, Marvin, I don't like what you're doing. *I am not your woman.* I'm not your lady."

"Since when?"

"Since you haven't bothered to call; since you can feel free to do with or without me; and since you're acting so silly. Allan is your friend as well as mine."

"No such thing as friendship between a man and a woman. If you're not my woman, whose woman are you?"

For the first time she was beginning to see through Marvin's selfishness. She had known all along that he took her love for granted, unconditionally; but she could not admit it before. "I'm my own woman," she said, trying to control her anger. "And I'll have you know, I'll dance with Allan, I'll dance with Gary, *I'll dance with anybody I please.*"

"Hey-y-y." He took her hands and tried to draw her to him.

She pushed him away. "It won't work this time, Marvin. I never interfered with you and your women because I have no claim on you. I loved you, but that gave you no claim over me."

"No, you *love* me, and I love you," he shouted, taking her hands.

"No, no, no!" She pulled away and went to find Allan and his friend.

They had already gone. She was glad she had given Gary her address and telephone number. She went to phone her mother, feeling more relieved than she had felt in a long time. There was no longer a need for her to be grateful to Marvin for nothing. The rest of the vacation should be easy. She sighed. Ahead of her was: getting back to school—and the challenge of Manning.

Thirteen

Emma moved quickly through the crowded gym, scanning names above stations to make sure she got the best teacher at the right time, for the right class. She was feeling buoyant, pleased with herself for the first time in a long while. The rejection she had faced recently had forced a retreat into herself to find what was lacking. Not beauty. Certainly not brain. Her grade report for the first semester at Manning showed a continuing four-point average. Letters and brochures were pouring in from colleges and universities. This outpouring bolstered her ego; she was sought after.

If she were lacking in anything, it was the will to do what *she* felt was best to do. The central fault, she realized, was that, as if by nature, she always tried to please everyone else, sometimes at the risk of her own happiness. Armed with that insight, she resolved to make this, her last semester of high school, count for her. She would think *Emma,* do her work, graduate, leave Manning, and start fresh in a place that wanted her.

Now with class cards in hand, she waded through the crowd looking for Mr. Wheeler, her choice for American literature. Mr. Wheeler, a young Black, had completed only one semester on the faculty at Manning. Although he was a newcomer, he was gaining a good reputation. Emma was anxious to get into his class because he was the only American lit teacher there who included Black writers in his course. Allan had warned that if she wanted him, she had better get there early.

Finally she reached his station. Teachers on both sides of him were busy signing cards while Mr. Wheeler sat drumming on the table with his pencil, a half-smile lighting his face; yet, he had a distracted look, oblivious of the hustle and bustle about him. What luck, Emma thought as she handed him her card. In the moment that he took to read her card, she was aware of his long slender fingers, his large blunt fingernails, well clipped and groomed but not manicured.

"I've filled my lit class," Mr. Wheeler said, handing her back her card.

"You wouldn't kid me now, would you, Mr. Wheeler?"

He laughed. "I most certainly would not. I'd be delighted to enroll you."

"Aw! Can't you take just one more?"

"Sorry about that. Now, Mr. Kooner may be able to take you."

Mr. Kooner sat right next to Mr. Wheeler. He glanced at Emma with a noncommittal look, then went on signing cards. Emma had a feeling he didn't want her any more than she wanted him. She must find Allan and get some advice.

Allan knew most of the teachers there by reputation. He could tell her what to do. Disappointed, she went looking for him. The crush was terrific. People were wall-to-wall. There was no escape from the odor of bodies, gym lockers, and shower stalls. Where was Allan?

She finally gave up and stumbled outside where the cold air was refreshing. Near the water fountain, Allan was having a hilarious time with Brenda and her friends. She hailed him. "There you are. I need you for a minute."

"Can't y' see we talkin' t' Allan?" Brenda demanded harshly.

"Excuse *me*. I was talking to *Allan*."

"I told y', *we* talkin'. Now if y' can't wait, then go on 'bout y' business."

Emma looked at Brenda. Brenda was indeed attractive. It was her fire, her eyes—big, black—in an oval, velvety-smooth black face. She was small, but had an ample bust, and the *real* hips that some girls at Marlborough bought to give that full-rounded look in jeans. How could such a pretty girl be so mean?

"Cool out, Bren, we aren't talking about nothing. Let me give Emma some time," Allan said and joined Emma.

Emma soon discovered that she had only two choices left for American lit: Mrs. Dohling and Mr. Kooner.

"Kooner is a dog," Allan said. "Why you taking lit?"

"I have to. It's the only required subject I haven't had. I saved it for now because it's easy. I want nothing to worry about this last semester. I'm juggling my schedule, Allan, trying to get a good lunch period."

"Fifth is best," Allan said.

"Can't have fifth."

"Then sixth. Whatever you do, don't take seventh. That's a drag."

"I won't get anything if I don't hurry," Emma said and rushed back to the gym.

The crush was even greater now as she pushed through to the English Department station, only to find that she was minutes late for Mrs. Dohling's class. It had just been filled. Oh, darn, she thought as she had to give in to letting Mr. Kooner sign her card.

To her dismay, his class was offered only at sixth period, forcing her to take seventh for lunch. At that time of day the food was like leftovers. Just to find space to stand and eat was impossible, and the sea gulls were then controlling the grounds. Despondent over her fate, she made her way toward the girls' rest room. Just outside she heard familiar voices and loud laughter.

When she walked in, there was a hush. The room was filled; Brenda, Liz, and the others were in the crowd. Brenda sat on the floor. The room reeked with tobacco and weed. Emma felt the ominous silence.

She washed her hands and had begun to comb her hair before the silence was interrupted.

"Some people 'round here think they such hot stuff they can come and call y' man while y' talkin' to 'im," Brenda said.

"Who tryin' to burn you, Brenda?" one girl asked.

"They know. Think they can come down here from the hills and take over."

Emma tossed her head as she combed her hair, trying hard to control the anger rising in her. She must not let Brenda get to her. She calmly took out her makeup.

"Aw, Brenda, you just making noise."

At that pronouncement, Emma glanced around and saw that the girl confronting Brenda was Carrie. Carrie was wearing a soft pink-and-white sweater dress, just above the knee, with a single strand of pearls that came almost to the hem of the dress. Her pearl earrings were also extra long. Exotic was the word for Carrie. Tall, thin, but big boned, Carrie could wear silver-streaked hair, silver nail polish, silver shoes, and white stockings and get away with it well.

"You stay outta this, Carrie," Brenda retorted.

"Bren, you know you ain't doing nothin' but talking stuff," Carrie said.

"She needn't think 'cause she from a 'nother part o' town her ass won't be kicked." Everybody laughed.

Emma bristled, then cautioned herself: Don't get in trouble with Brenda. Just one more semester. But could she continue to ignore knowing that Brenda had chosen her as a target? Could Carrie be right? Was Brenda just making noise? Emma thought, Maybe I should take a long shot, call Brenda's bluff, and settle it once and for all.

Carrie went on, "Aw, Brenda, shut up. Everybody in here knows if any ass is kicked, it would be yours." Everybody cracked up.

Emma suddenly realized that at the moment she need not take any risk. She gathered up her things, and with shoulders down, head high, quickly catching a wink from Carrie, she walked briskly from the room.

She went to find Allan, remembering the incident with Brenda after the game and how the showdown was averted by her mother. Then by Carrie today. She wished she had the gift to really understand people—*really understand them.* She knew why Brenda made her bristle, but why had Carrie come to her defense? But was it her defense or Carrie's offense?

On past the water fountain she went, still wondering how Brenda could be so mean. What was she lacking? It certainly wasn't beauty. Was she jealous? Of what? Could there be something going between her and Allan?

Suddenly Emma remembered what Marvin had said to Allan—". . . from the ghetto, taking over" —and Brenda's words about the "hills" had been similar. How stupid, she thought, claiming territory. Why couldn't she and Allan be friends? Did Brenda, too, believe there was no such thing as friendship between boys and girls, men and women?

Finally she saw Allan near the hash line, eating a sweet roll. She realized she was hungry. She must grab a bite and corner him for talk. He must know that besides the challenge of Brenda and the survivors she now also had the challenge of Kooner. Then, too, there was Carrie. Had she acquired a friend? She hailed Allan and rushed toward him.

Whether Carrie was friend or foe, she had hinted that Brenda was just a showoff, a big bluffer. Emma would store this information. It might be useful at a more crucial moment. But why all this worry about Brenda? she thought. Kooner may pose a greater challenge.

Fourteen

Fifth period ended a few minutes before the bell, so Emma had time to get to her locker between classes. She wanted to put away Gary's last letter from Stanford. Having Gary's letters helped ease the pain of not seeing Marvin. She wished Allan was around so that she could share a line or two with him. Why was Allan not at school today? she wondered. Then she recalled that he had been acting a bit cool lately.

When he said anything at all, it was about his mother's inability to find work, or about his looking for a part-time job and being unable to find anything. She now remembered his saying "We have nothing. If something doesn't give, I'll have to do something crazy." He had looked at her and as though he was angry, he said, "But what do you know about having nothing?" and walked away. Maybe he had quit school. Suddenly she realized, with horror, that she didn't know where he lived, nor did she have his telephone number.

She opened her locker, then quickly unfolded the pages of Gary's letter. She smiled as she read: *"Stanford is an OK place. It could be great if a lovely lady like you were around. Consider coming here, OK?"*

She scribbled on her notepad: *So you think I can make it at Stanford. I doubt it. That white sea is wider there than at Marlborough. I've had it with honkies.*

She was interrupted when a voice behind her exclaimed, "Hey, ain't that Marvin Richards? How you rate a picture of him?"

Emma looked up, wishing she had removed Marvin's picture from inside her locker door as she had planned. "Oh, hi, Carrie." She put the letter away. "Marvin and I went to the same school."

"You mean you went to Marlborough? Then you know Melanie Foster."

"Yeah, I know Melanie."

"Melanie is my cousin, know that?"

"No, I didn't know that," Emma said.

"Yeah. She and her mother would like not knowing it, too." Carrie laughed, wrapping her long, full black cape around her. "Her mother is so saditty, she don't wanta have nothing to do with us. And she's my mama's sister, girl."

Emma, embarrassed by this openness, averted her eyes as Carrie rushed on.

"Now Melanie's father, he's OK, really a nice man. But Melanie, she don't hardly ever see him. He works *three* jobs, girl, to keep his woman in style. But Melanie's mama is off her wig; and poor Melanie —she's a trip."

Why was Carrie telling her all of this? Emma smiled and said, "Thanks for putting Brenda down for me."

"Oh, that. 'Twas nothing. She's always scoping for trouble, knowing she can't handle it when she finds it. Forgit her." Carrie swooped off, letting her black cape float. Emma watched her saunter down the hall in soft red leather folding boots—one up, the other down. Today each fingernail was a different color. Emma laughed. Carrie is a trip herself, she thought.

The bell rang. The crowd poured out of rooms into the already crowded hall. Emma hurriedly ripped Marvin's picture down and reluctantly walked upstairs to face Mr. Kooner. In the hallway, students were clanging locker doors trying to beat the second bell, while Mr. Wheeler urged people on to class. Seeing him, she thought of Allan. What would she do if Allan did not come back?

Mr. Wheeler quickly stepped aside for Emma and said, "Smile!"

Emma tried to respond.

"Much better." He smiled back.

Mr. Kooner was sitting behind the desk that held two piles of books: nine in one, eight in the other. He glanced up at Emma. The look did not wish her a good afternoon. She knew Mr. Kooner was aware that she had enrolled in his class only because she had no other choice.

James, the big football lineman and a student council officer, came in and sat close to the teacher's desk. "You oughta let us off today, Mr. Kooner."

"Take off," Mr. Kooner said matter-of-factly. "Any day you like."

Latecomers straggled in, laughing and joking with Mr. Kooner, whose manner was never ruffled by their lateness. He just sat. Was it condescension? And was all this laughing and joking an apology for his lack of attention and concern? Allan's toms, she thought. She wished she could leave that room and never come back.

Don came in and sat beside Emma. Don was pleasant. He was thin, tall, and dark, his face sprinkled with pimples. His pants were always too short. It was as if Don's body defied harnessing. Today, not only were his pants too short, they were very tight.

A burst of laughter and loud talking ushered in Liz, who was delivered to class by Brenda and her crowd. The gum popping sounded like fireworks as Liz looked around for a choice seat.

Carrie and Walt entered last. These two walked

in, hand in hand, and headed down front. Carrie had discarded her cape. She wore a tight beige skirt and a low-cut red sweater. She and Walt moved as if they were listening to music arranged just for them. The sound of horns and the roll of drums could be heard in the sway of Carrie's walk.

Today Walt looked as he always looked: as if he had just stepped from the pages of GQ. He was wearing a deep-purple, (almost black) wool coat; a lavender, shetland wool sweater; a white shirt and a deep-purple tie with a thin, cross stripe, the same color as the sweater. He must go to the hairdresser before school, Emma guessed, for his perm was always just right. It was rumored his mother paid him a salary for attending school.

"Hey, Walt," someone shouted from the back of the room. "Somebody's burning y', man. Moving in on y' time. Check it out."

Walt jerked around. Carrie placed her long slim fingers coolly on Walt's arm. She looked at the caller. "Shut your mouth, jackass. Y' just mad 'cause I don't mess 'round with you." She steered Walt to their seats.

Mr. Kooner waited; he watched this small drama with a bemused look on his tanned face. Carrie and Walt set the stage for his deep, clear, dramatic voice. "Now that the little bedroom scene is over, we will turn our minds to higher things."

Emma raised her hand. "Mr. Kooner, may I,

please, hold a book today?" There were only seventeen books for thirty-five students.

"That's left up to you entirely, Ms. Walsh. Your chance of holding a book is as good as anyone else's in the room. I see to that. No one can say I do not believe in equality of opportunity."

He walked from behind the desk and looked over the room. Then he turned to the sixteen books. "All right, get ready." He pushed the books to the floor and the scramble was on.

The laughter, pushing, and jostling turned the scramble into a scrimmage. Emma sat appalled by this behavior, adamant, refusing to join in.

Don rushed for a book and in the rough and tumble split his pants. He wore no underwear and his behind was exposed. Fingers pointed as gales of laughter rang out. Emma looked at the teacher, then at Don, whose dark face had turned ashen gray. He eased into a nearby seat. A peculiar look spread over his face, almost a grin, painful without the usual signs of pain—a vacant expression, like that of someone who is unknowingly bleeding to death.

Emma felt crushed, humiliated. That look on Don's face would, she knew, forever be stamped on her memory. And so would the look on the teacher's. Mr. Kooner had not laughed. But the contempt Emma had seen on his face was worse than laughter. What was he thinking? she wondered.

Finally the class settled down and Kooner directed their attention to the text. But before they could begin to work, the bell sounded the end of the class period.

Emma left the room, remembering the look on Don's face. Something has to be done about that Mr. Kooner, she thought angrily. But what? And who would do what had to be done?

Fifteen

It was pouring rain as Emma's mother drove down the hill to the east side of town. Streets were flooded, and at times Emma thought the motor would die. Her mother handled the car with assurance. Emma stared out at the falling rain and wished the day had been declared an official rainy day and no school. She could stand a day without Kooner.

She looked at her mother, who was dressed for the rainy weather, and thought how different she was these days. She smiled more. She acted like one who could combine suffering and pleasure and emerge strong.

Her mother caught Emma's eye and smiled. "Why you looking at me like that?"

Emma smiled back. "I like seeing you the way you are."

"How am I?"

"I don't know. But you look happy. Is it because you know I'll soon be gone?"

"Oh, Emma. Not that you'll be gone. But I am happy that you're almost ready to go."

"All I have to do now is make up my mind. I might go to Stanford."

"Because of that Gary? I thought you would go to the same school as Marvin. What's with you and him?"

"Nothing, Mama." She did not want to talk about Marvin with her mother. It seemed that her mother leaned toward Marvin.

"There's something."

"It certainly isn't anything that would change my mind about what school I'll attend."

Emma thought, It was you who warned me to be careful of being grateful for nothing. I'm merely taking your advice. Marvin's not for me and that's that. But all she said was, "Marvin has lots of women. He'll be fine without me."

"The question is, will you be fine without him? He's nice and warm and friendly. He's gonna go far, too. I don't know if you'll find anyone any better than Marvin."

Emma sighed and turned away with her chin on her hand and listened to the pour of the rain and the swish-swash, swish-swash of the windshield wipers.

She thought of Gary's answer to her last letter, still urging her to consider Stanford: *"You have your stuff together, lady. Just to be aware enough to raise the question of racism puts you way ahead. Remember: To swim in this vast white sea toughens you for that vaster white shore. . . ."* But her mother need not know that.

Before getting out of the car she opened her umbrella, then made a dash for the main building. The rain had made her later than usual. The hall was already crowded. She was glad she had extra socks in her locker. The ones she had on were soaking even in that short distance.

As she changed her socks, she wondered if Allan would brave the rain—if he were coming back. He was too close to graduating and had too much going for him to quit now. She looked at the crowd going and coming, squirming in place like a mass of worms. She asked herself, Do they know how alone I feel here, how out of place? She remembered the day Liz had tapped her on the shoulder. How mistaken she had been to think Liz had singled her out for friendship. Brenda had evidently put Liz up to inviting her over, hoping that Emma would give in, take the insults, and become one of Brenda's followers. *No way,* she thought. Then she saw Allan.

Filled with irrepressible delight, she pushed through the crowd to reach him. He was moving away from her; she was losing him. "Allan, Allan!" she called out. He did not hear her. "Touch him," she shouted to James, who was near Allan, looking at her struggling. James responded and Allan stopped.

Out of breath, she almost whispered, "Hi, where were you yesterday?"

"I wasn't here," he said, not nearly matching her enthusiasm.

"Allan, I know that. Where were you?" she asked with friendly emphasis.

"At home." He let her know by his somber mood he was not going to tell her more.

"Man, you were so right. That Kooner is a dog." She brought him up to date on the scramble. He said nothing. She then tried another approach: She told about Carrie's show of friendship. "Why you think she'd tell me about her family, Allan? Isn't that weird, she doesn't know me *that* well."

Allan looked at her still, not saying anything. She told him about the latest letter from Gary. Finally she said, "Allan, what's wrong with you? You're not even listening to me, man."

He hit his palm with his fist. "So you have problems, eh?" He looked at her and his mouth quivered. For a moment she didn't know whether he was angry or going to cry. He said no more. She waited.

Allan sighed. He looked at Emma, "So you want to know why I wasn't here yesterday. I had to be home so the social worker could see a live body before she'd hand over some food stamps. They say it doesn't git cold in California. That's a lie. When the heat's off, it's cold, Em." There was an ominous silence. Allan's voice was almost a whisper. "The worker asked what we had in the house. I knew what we had, exactly. But when my mother said 'salt and flour,' something snapped inside of me and I had to go some to keep from asking that lady to get out of our house. Probably, you're wondering, now, why I'm telling you all of this, talking like Carrie *talked*. You don't understand. You don't have all that shit that has to come out, or blow your mind."

Emma lowered her eyes. She could not bear to look at him. She thought of the anger she had felt when Danny had suggested her as a resource for welfare information. Now she burned with shame that she had reacted so angrily—not only because Danny had assumed that because she was *Black* she automatically knew, but mostly because she, at the time, felt herself above such knowledge. She wanted to tell Allan this, how she felt, now. But what could she say? She wanted to reach out, take his hand, and tell him she did understand, but she just stood there with her head down.

It was as though he sensed her dilemma; he took her hand. "It's OK, we'll be all right."

"Allan, give me your phone number."

"I'll give you my address. I don't have a phone."

No phone? Everybody has a phone, she thought. To her a phone was like heat, like light, a necessity. Suddenly she realized that maybe Allan was right: She did not understand *his* meaning of nothing.

"Now what's this about Kooner? I knew he was

a dog, but not that kind of dog." Allan was himself again.

She looked up at him. He was a good person, a real friend. A warm feeling spread over her. It was that same feeling she often sensed when she wished for a brother. She now knew what it was like to have a brother; and if she ever had a real one, she would want him to be like Allan.

The morning went by without the rain letting up. There was no spill over of the crowd outside so the hallways were packed. It was impossible to open a locker without assaulting or being assaulted. One would have thought that rain would have increased absenteeism, but it seemed those who were usually absent took refuge from home in the crowded halls.

Emma stepped around people eating lunch to get to Kooner's class, hardly able to wait for seventh period she was so hungry. She hoped there would still be a decent hot dog left when she reached the lunch counter.

Immediately after the second bell Mr. Kooner started reading announcements: "For seniors only, SAT tests—"

"What's SAT, Mr. Kooner?" someone interrupted.

"You a senior?"

"Naw."

"Well, it doesn't concern you. The test will be

held again soon. More info on that in the office."

Emma listened, knowing that she and James were the only seniors in the class as Kooner read on: "*In this school, three speakers and three alternates are chosen for the graduation exercise. Any senior may turn in a paper for the competition to his/her English or history teacher.*" Emma felt a surge of excitement. Should she compete? If only she were at Marlborough. There would be no question.

Mr. Kooner then came from behind his desk, walking the aisles with a small notepad. When all the latecomers had arrived he started in assigning seats. "James and Ms. Flower." Everybody laughed. He was insuring Ms. Flower, the smallest person in the class, access to a book.

Emma was surprised when he left Don beside her. Don had continued to scramble each day in spite of the humiliation he had suffered. It was as though he had to avoid the thought of not being up to the fray. Or as a driver who had suffered an accident, he had to get right back under the wheel or risk losing the courage to drive again. Was Kooner insuring her a book? Emma wondered. Or was he merely making sure she witnessed an example of the "good" student?

When the seat changes were made, the scramble was on. Walt and James went for the same book. Walt grabbed first, clutching the book close to his fine suede leather jacket. James tried to take the book but instead got hold of Walt's jacket, pulling the button through the fabric. Walt hit James in the neck and a fight was on. There was bedlam.

Emma kept her eyes on the teacher, who had a look of wild excitement and a peculiar grin on his face. Emma touched Don. "Look at the teacher, look at the teacher," she cried. Suddenly there was silence and everybody was looking at Mr. Kooner, having heard Emma.

Emma's heart leaped with terror when Mr. Kooner braced his shoulders, put on a stern face, and looked in her direction.

"What did you say?" he asked.

Emma lowered her eyes and said nothing.

"What did she say, Mr. Armstrong?" Mr. Kooner asked Don.

"I don't know, Mr. Kooner," Don answered and wiggled in his seat.

Emma had the urge to speak up, but could not say a word.

"What did she say?" Mr. Kooner punctuated every word.

"I told y'. I don't know." Don was uncomfortable.

"Think you can remember in the V.P.'s office?"

Emma became alarmed. "I'll tell you, Mr. Kooner," she said shyly.

"No, I asked him. What did she say, Mr. Armstrong?"

Don looked at Emma and rolled his eyes and

pouted his lips. "She said you like seein' us fightin'."

The tension was broken by loud laughter. Kooner seemed appeased, and the class settled down for the lesson that was almost immediately interrupted by the bell.

Emma touched Don's sleeve as they entered the crowded hall. "I'm so sorry Mr. Kooner took it out on you, Don." She could not bring herself to look at Don, she was so ashamed.

Don kept moving as he said, "That's OK, but next time you better git your word in first."

Emma pushed through the crowd, angry and humiliated. She hated herself for getting into trouble with Kooner. What if he did make them scramble; everybody else saw it as fun. Why couldn't she? But it was just after midterm and they had finished work by only three authors. She felt she was wasting time.

Near the exit to the cafeteria, Brenda, Liz, and their little group were holding forth. As Emma approached she heard Liz say, "Ms. Saddity think she know so much, almost got Don put outta class. We can do without smarties like that."

Emma burned with shame. She had expected Don to be angry at her, but she had hoped, at least, the others would have understood that it was *Kooner* who had taken it out on Don. She knew she must be careful. She was isolated enough. She didn't need thirty-five students down on her. Maybe she should brave the scramble and win their goodwill, she thought, and joined the long cafeteria line in the rain.

By the time she reached the serving counter, her hunger had changed from a keen desire awakened by odors and imaginings of good things to a dull stomachache. Seeing what was left did little to arouse the earlier appetite. All the hot dogs were gone. Hamburger patties lay on the tray like small mounds of leather. The casserole of noodles and more noodles was now pasty and the salads were withered.

She settled for a hamburger and almost decided to pass up the relish when she saw mustard in the mayonnaise, onions in the pickle relish, and catsup spread all over. Managing to secure milk and a piece of cake, she looked around. There was no place to sit or stand in the crowded cafeteria. How would she manage with her umbrella and tray to get back into the building in the rain? She would have to do without the umbrella.

Wind gusts swept the rain in waves. She waited. The rain lessened. She made a dash for the building. Suddenly there was a flutter and flapping around her. She screamed, dropped the tray, her food scattering over the soggy grounds. Then she saw the scrawny sea gull winging away with her hamburger in his beak, his murky body quickly camouflaged in the gray, misty clouds and rain.

Boiling with rage, her first reaction was to retrieve what she could. She picked up the milk and saw the cake disintegrate. Suddenly she heard laughter and looked toward the building. The door was open and a crowd had gathered in the doorway, laughing at her.

All the shame, guilt, and degradation she had felt that day seemed to crowd in on her, pelting her like the rain. This violence that was done in the name of "fun" was overwhelming. She flung the tray and the soggy remnants away and screamed at the crowd, "I hate this place. I hate you and everything here." Her voice cracked with tears as she screamed, "You are all a bunch of stupid idiots." She knew it did no good. They couldn't even hear her for she was drowned out by the laughter and the rain.

Sixteen

*Emma's clothes were still damp and her senses out-*raged by the time her mother picked her up. "I hate this place," she said, settling in the car. "I wish I never had to come back, ever."

"What happened, Emma?"

"I can't stand that Mr. Kooner."

"Now we're not going through that. You have only one semester and you'll no longer need Mr. Kooner."

"But, Mama, you don't know what he's doing to us." After she had told her mother about the incidents, knowing her mother would be outraged, she said, "We ought to do something about this."

"We'll see to it that you get a book."

"But, Mama, everybody has a right to a book. Mr. Kooner should see to that. I bet no teacher at Marlborough could get away with that."

"Now, maybe you can see why we wanted you at Marlborough."

"But Ma—"

"You take care of *Emma,* OK? You'll get your book, get your work, and you leave the rest to the principal, or somebody else. Books for everybody is not your concern."

How could she show up with a book? The others in the class would certainly laugh at her. She was having trouble enough. And what would Mr. Kooner say? However, she knew it would do no good to try convincing her mother that something else must be done.

That evening she tried to put her mind on her homework, but she could not concentrate. Kooner, Eoil Can, and those people in the doorway laughing kept coming back to make her miserable. There must be someone at that school, other than Allan, that she could go to for help. Maybe Mr. Wheeler. What could he do? He was too new to make waves. The principal was the person to tell. But how could she tell the principal something like that? Surely he must know already. Maybe she should tell her daddy. He just might go and talk to Mr. Kooner. If only she knew what to do.

Get hold, she told herself. Go along and it will soon be over. Maybe she would scramble, but she would never eat in that cafeteria again. She would take her lunch and find a place away from them all. They would not have her to laugh at again. She could see the fingers pointing, hear the laughter, feel the cold rain. The humiliation overwhelmed her. She gave up trying to study and went to bed. Still restless, she got up and wrote to Gary: *There's a white tiger loose, controlling my American Lit. class. He has us tearing one another apart just for a book. Nobody seems to care enough to stand with me and say a soft "no." But enough of that. It's prom time! How about coming down for that event? Can you say a strong "yes" to that? Please do.*

The next morning the sky was a deep blue, the air cold and clear. Mountains, usually hidden by smog, loomed in the distance like sleeping dinosaurs. A perfect day, Emma thought. If only she were heading someplace other than Manning.

She and her mother did not talk. Why didn't her mother understand? Emma looked at the book on her lap and the anger returned. She recalled the scene with her mother that morning.

"I don't want to take that book. I can just hear them when I show with a book from the library."

"What do you care what they say? You're there to learn, not to please them."

"We can only keep this book for two weeks, then what'll we do?"

"By then we'll have bought a book."

"I'm not going to take it."

"You *are,* and that's that. I don't want to hear any more about books and Mr. Kooner."

No use talking to her, Emma thought. She shifted the book, knowing she would never show up in class with it unless everyone else had a book, too.

She said good-bye to her mother without having reconciled. More despair: Allan was not waiting in the usual place. His habits had changed greatly since the social worker's visit. He seemed absorbed in other things now. He was often late, even for class. He seemed not to listen any more, nor to care about anything. If only he were the old Allan, able to give her advice.

The grounds were quiet. A few puddles were left rippling in the wind. A blade of grass here and there held a raindrop that sparkled like a diamond— orange and blue streaks from a brilliant white light. Emma wanted to touch them, but knew one touch and all that sparkle would disappear.

The custodian moved down the walk with a long-handled broom, making short, swift sweeps. His khaki pants and shirt gleamed with starch, his black bow tie neatly in place. His shoes were highly polished. Does he have kids? Emma wondered. Did he live with them? Bet he does. Maybe she should talk to him about Kooner. She had a great urge to go over and interrupt his sweeping, but the urge quickly faded.

Four police cars gunned by without sirens. What

had happened? She wished Allan would come. The crowd gathered slowly.

James hurried up the steps. "Hi. How's Ms. Walsh today?"

"OK. Where're you rushing?"

"To council."

"Say, wait a minute." She suddenly had an idea. "You think the council could do something about Kooner?"

"What's wrong with Kooner?"

"The scramble—our not having enough books." She was surprised at the question.

"Oh, that." James laughed. "I doubt it. Why don't you come talk to 'em this morning and see?"

Only eleven of the twenty members were in the council hall. Even Ms. Dohling, their sponsor, had not arrived. James introduced Emma to the president, Cynthia White, who was a tall, dark, heavy girl. The left side of her face, neck, and her left arm were scarred. Cindy, as the others called her, appeared self-assured, pleasant, articulate. She was head girl in her class, elected by the student body to the council.

Emma told why she had come. They all were attentive. "Yeah," Cindy said, "that's Mr. Kooner, all right. Unfortunately, student council can't deal with teachers. We can only do little things like raise money, handle some minor student things, and advise students who to see when they're in trouble."

"That's something for parents to handle," one girl said.

"That's a problem for Mr. Freeman, our dear principal," James said.

"Fine. If he were ever here." Cindy looked at Emma and smiled. "I'm gonna tell you like it is. All we can do is suggest that you live with Mr. Kooner, or have your parents come and take care of it."

Emma left feeling she had gotten nowhere. She should use the book her mother had gotten from the library and forget it. She hurried to her first class to beat the second bell.

The morning went by without her having seen Allan, and too soon the dreaded sixth period arrived. Should she cut class, go to the library? She had to have a pass to go to the library during class periods. Where could she go? She wished she could go home. If only there was a way on and off campus without a pass. The bell rang. She had to make up her mind. She would face Kooner, but she *would not* take that book.

The room was empty. Was Kooner absent? Her anticipation of a substitute teacher was short-lived. Mr. Kooner entered and the silence between them was ominous. Should she wait outside for the others to arrive?

Just then James came in with his usual banter.

"Say, Mr. Kooner, I was thinking about being one of them speakers at graduation. 'Where Do We Go From Here?' Now I could talk awhile on that subject."

"Really," Kooner said, laughing. "I never thought of you as one of the few around here that looks beyond the moment."

The stinging comment mixed with laughter angered Emma and she decided that she would enter the competition and turn her paper in to Mr. Kooner.

The second bell brought in others, laughing and joking; latecomers sauntered in as usual as if they were ahead of time. What made them come? Emma wondered. Strange, no one was ever absent from this class. Would it have made a difference? Would the scramble have ended if that odd person had stayed away? Could it be the scramble that made them come? What was that excitement that drove them on while she sat humiliated? The unreal laughter, that strange force that made them delight in hurting; why didn't they turn on Kooner and protect each other?

Her mind ran to graduation. Who would be valedictorian at Marlborough? Her chances to have been were excellent. She thought of Dee and Cheryl, of Marvin. They all would be graduating. She wished she was back at her old school, away from Kooner. Then she thought, forget Marlborough. For better or worse, Manning is my school.

The scramble was over and the teacher was standing beside her. His voice startled her.

"Pick up that paper around this desk. I cannot work in this clutter."

She looked up, but did not move.

"I'm talking to you, Ms. Walsh."

Her first impulse was to pick up the paper. "I didn't put that paper there." The words surprised her. There was silence.

"Whether you did or not, pick it up."

"I put that paper there." Liz, who was sitting just behind Emma, moved to pick up the paper.

"No. Ms. Walsh will do it."

Emma stiffened with anger. Pick up the paper and don't tangle with the man, she told herself; but she could not bring herself to bend to do it. The silence thickened.

"I'm waiting."

Her back straightened, Emma lifted her head and turned her face away and stared straight ahead. The silence was now foreboding.

"All right, Ms. Walsh. You may leave the room. Don't come back until you have a permit slip."

"That's cold," somebody muttered.

Emma quickly left the room. The anger swelled in her throat, tears blinded her. *Why couldn't she pick up that paper?* What would she say to the vice-principal?

"Hey." Allan rushed after her, keeping his voice almost in a whisper. "Wait up. Where you going?"

She turned around, but could not say a word as the tears flowed.

"What's the matter, Em?" he asked, alarmed.

She struggled to control the tears. Finally she said, "Oh, Allan, I'm angry, angry, angry. I could destroy that man. He put me out of class because I wouldn't pick up paper."

"You should be happy."

"Please, Allan. I'll have to see the V.P. before I can get back in there."

"For not picking up paper?" Allan laughed. "The V.P. will think he's off his wig, sending you in for that. Here they put you out for smoking dope, for a holdup, assault. You'll get a permit, don't worry."

Her worry doubled when she discovered that the girl's vice-principal and the boy's vice-principal were away at a special meeting. She would have to see the principal. She waited and listened as a group of boys caught smoking weed tried to implicate one who swore he had walked into the boy's toilet just before the teacher who reported the incident.

"Aw, Ted, you know y' wuz." A voice was followed by a snicker.

"I wasn't. Smell my breath, Mr. Freeman. I don't smoke nothing."

That must be Ted pleading, Emma thought. Laughter came from the inner office.

"I don't want to hear any more until I see you with your parents." The booming voice startled Emma. "Out!"

"But, Mr. Freeman," Ted cried.

"Out, I said. Bring your parents."

Four boys came out, three snickering, pointing fingers at Ted, cracking up. Ted was scowling, boiling with rage, yet helpless against their trickery.

Emma remembered the day in the rain with Eoil Can and felt anguished. What if she were told to bring her mother? Her hands began to perspire; she couldn't sit still, so great was the urge to escape.

Suddenly she had an idea: Put Kooner down. Tell the principal about the scramble. Her spirit lifted, but despair returned when the tall, robust, ruddy-complexioned man asked her to come into the office. She had heard that Mr. Freeman was an ex-marine, ex-football coach, who was stern. Everybody was glad he wasn't around often.

"What can I do for you, young lady?" he asked matter-of-factly.

"I need a permit slip to return to Mr. Kooner's class."

"Just like that: You want a permit slip. . . ."

"I have to . . . Well, you see, he asked me to pick up some paper . . . but it wasn't just that. He makes us scramble for books and I . . . I just can't do it."

The laughter surprised Emma. "All those big boys in there; a good-looking girl like you shouldn't have to scramble. Let them scramble for you!"

She couldn't believe it. She had the permit in her hand and the word that Mr. Kooner was one of the finest teachers in the school. Something was wrong.

She was wrong. She could hear her mother complaining: *Emma, you're always making a mountain out of a molehill.* Still she knew that the humiliation, anger, and anguish she felt doing the scramble was real. There had to be someone who would understand. She would call her father.

·

Seventeen

The waiter set a huge iced bowl of shrimp in the center of the table, placed menus, and retreated. The cocktail waitress quickly followed.

Emma's father looked up. "A double martini for the lady . . ."

"Ladies?" the waitress asked, looking from Jody to Emma.

"Oh, no, she's not eighteen." He glanced at Emma.

"I will be soon," Emma retorted, a scowl in her voice.

"Wine for me. Emma, Seven-Up?"

Emma refused the Seven-Up and took nothing to drink before dinner. She squirmed as the old insecurity she felt with her father returned. Here she was almost eighteen, feeling as incapable as a six-year-old. If only she knew how to cope with Kooner, she wouldn't be at this table.

The menu was of little interest. She knew she would order crab legs, her favorite, but she didn't feel hungry. Why had her father chosen a fancy restaurant at the marina for their talk? Any hamburger place with just the two of them would have been fine.

Emma glanced at Jody. The candlelight flickered and caught the fire in Jody's ring as she flipped the shells off the fresh pink shrimp. Her imported, bottle-green dress was perfect with her light hair and gray eyes. Jody caught Emma's eye and smiled. Emma quickly looked away.

"Em, I take it you need help with your resume and applications to colleges," her father said.

"Oh, no. That's done."

He was obviously surprised. "Have you already settled on a school?"

"Not really, but I've narrowed them down to three: Meharry, Howard, and Stanford.

"Meharry? Howard? Never heard of those schools," Jody said.

"They're Black medical schools: Howard is in D.C., Meharry is in Tennessee. I can understand Howard and Meharry; but with all that Black togetherness lately, why Stanford?" her father wanted to know.

"Maybe I'm ready to test some of the things I'm learning about myself." Emma grinned. "A friend suggested the idea, and I like it." She then told of her plans to write a paper for the graduation speakers' competition.

"So you think you have something profound to say about the future?" her father asked.

"I do. So much it's hard to know just where to start. There's the idea of peace and liberation, pollution, whether we'll go on living. There's a lot to say, but who will listen?"

"I'm open," Jody said.

"I'll listen if you have a meaningful plan of action," her father said.

"I'm working on it in my own way." Emma was pleased with the response.

Her father smiled and said, "You seem to have things well in hand; what else is there to talk about?"

This is it, she thought. Now she would have to give the real reason why she had asked to talk to him. She looked out at the sparkling waters and wished she had not asked at all. If only her mother had shown courage and talked to Kooner. She sighed, "Daddy, I . . ." She sighed again. "I'm having trouble with this teacher."

"Not again. You just got to that school. Are you in for another transfer?"

Emma lowered her head. "Please." Then she quickly glanced at Jody. How much did Jody know about her problems? Why does she have to be here? Finally, she said, "No. It's just that I need somebody to talk to him. He's mean; he's really no teacher. He doesn't care—"

"Wait," her father interrupted, "all you're saying is he doesn't like you. Does it matter whether he likes you? He doesn't have to like you. He just has to teach you."

"Aw, you don't understand. . . ."

"Help me understand."

The waiter interrupted to take their orders, giving Emma time to think of what she would say. When the waiter left, she went straight to the point. "Mr. Kooner makes us scramble for books like animals over scraps."

"What do you mean, scramble?" her father demanded.

Emma explained exactly what Kooner did and how the reactions of the students compounded her humiliation.

"Now I see the problem," her father said. Silver gleamed in the light and the glass sparkled as her father sipped the amber wine.

Can he imagine, even, those scenes with Kooner? Emma wondered. She pushed the food aimlessly around on her plate. Crab legs that usually made her mouth water and her fingers eager to get at them did not arouse her appetite. Finally she asked, "So, you'll talk to him?"

"Why do I need to talk to him? The problem is you need a book." He laid a fifty-dollar bill near Emma's plate. "This should get what you need."

"That's not the problem," she shouted.

"Hey, remember where you are," her father cautioned.

She burned with shame, but she was still angry when she lowered her voice. "*Mr. Kooner* is the problem and somebody needs to do something about him."

"He's not *your* problem. You're a good enough student to work without a teacher, Emma. You get your book and do your work, pass your exams, and get the hell out of there."

She had been failed again. She believed her father would understand her humiliation and, at least, talk to Mr. Kooner. Why were her parents so unwilling to let Kooner know he was responsible for finding the books that the schools provided for them? The old feeling of rejection she knew so well when she was with her father welled up inside her. She could never depend upon him to help when she needed him most. Money!

She picked up the fifty-dollar bill and handed it back. "This won't do. Can't you see? I can't walk into class with a book."

"I don't understand why you are so upset," her father said.

"Maybe Emma should be upset," Jody said.

"I think you should stay out of this." Her father

gave Jody a glowering look. "I don't intend to get drawn into a situation where the students themselves don't seem to care."

"They can't do any more than I can," Emma cried.

"You either buy yourself a book, or live with that teacher." Her father pushed the money toward her.

She thrust the money back. "I'll not buy a book, that's for sure. And I don't think scrambling is something I can live with."

The only sound was the tinkling of silver on china as Jody and Emma's father finished their meal. Emma sat stonily looking at her plate. Why couldn't she do what everybody else thought was the right thing: Get her own book or go along with the other students? Everybody else could not be wrong.

The money still lay near her father's plate. All she had to do was reach for it. Maybe the heavy tension would be relieved and she could enjoy her dinner. But she could not bring herself to pick it up and clear the air. She sat trying to control the feeling of outrage.

Later that evening she tried to work on the graduation speech, make more notes, improve the first few pages. No use. Her mind would not focus on work.

Finally she lay in bed trying to forget the scene in the restaurant. Why had she asked anything of her father? She should have known he would find his solution and ignore whatever she said. But could he be right? Was she being stubborn? Could anybody put Kooner down when the students enjoyed the scramble?

She tossed and turned, unable to sleep. She could see the class poised—some on the edge of their seats—waiting for the signal. Was it because they loved to read? She turned over angrily and said aloud, "Couldn't be." What made them do it? Suddenly she felt that the answer might be that nobody had told them they shouldn't. Maybe they believed it was the thing to do because it was fun.

Should she tell them how she felt? Would they listen? She thought of Liz and the day the teacher had attacked Don. Certainly Liz would not listen. James was convinced there was nothing students could do; Don—out of the question. Maybe Carrie. She wished she could forget Kooner and fall asleep.

Sleep would not come. She thought about her father again. If only he would do something. She could see him, self-assured, walking into Kooner's class, polite but firm, demanding a stop to the scramble. Wouldn't Kooner be surprised? All the students would want to know, who is that man? What would they think when they learned that he was her father, declaring scrambling had no place in their school?

Don't be silly, she told herself. Come to your senses, act your age, and forget him. Put him out of your life. The fullness now all the way into her throat forced tears into her eyes when she realized she was still kidding herself. *She'd never forget her father.* She loved him too much and had to go on loving him. She fought the tears and willed herself not to succumb to self-pity. He is as he is, she told herself. She must learn to love him as he is and not expect him to help her solve her problems. She felt better as she slowly counted backward from two hundred.

Eighteen

A loud knock on the door startled her out of deep sleep. She would have to hurry. That there was no time to make her lunch for school frustrated her and she wished she could stay home.

"Get your things together and let's get out of here," her mother demanded. "You're making me late."

"I have my things."

"Where's the book I got you from the library?"

"I'm not taking it."

"Aren't you going to class?" Her mother was impatient.

"I'm just not taking the book, Mama." Emma tried to control her anger.

"Emma, what's the matter with you? You don't seem satisfied unless you're getting into trouble. Get that book now, so we can go."

"Mama, *I'm not taking it.*"

"*You are taking it.*"

Emma knew she had backed herself into a corner. How would she ever get out? She could take the book and leave it in her locker, but that would not solve the problem with her mother. She had to let her mother know exactly how she felt, but now she was frightened. Maybe she had gone too far. "I always do what *you* want done. Why can't you see that I have to do something that *I* think is right sometime?"

"I don't have time to argue with you, girl."

"Then don't. Just listen. I'll soon be old enough to vote—deciding who will be the President of these United States. Why can't I decide whether I want to take a book to school or not?"

"It's not just taking a book to school and you know it. But I don't have time for this. Don't take the book, and if you get into trouble, don't come to me. If you think you're old enough to make your choices, please be old enough to live with them, responsibly."

They rode in silence. Although Emma was relieved that she had put her mother on notice, she was still worried and uncertain. She had no idea what she was going to do. She knew she didn't want to leave her mother feeling anxious and tense. She wanted to say that she would not do anything foolish; but how could she say that? She was not sure of anything.

As the car pulled alongside the curb she felt a moment of fear and wished she had brought the book. No turning back now. "Mama, I'm glad you left it up to me. It's time I live with what I decide to do." She leaned over and kissed her mother's cheek. "Hope with me that I don't do anything foolish, something not worth living with."

The second bell had sounded before she slipped into first period unnoticed as the teacher readmitted students absent the day before. Now she had time to be angry at herself for sleeping late. She did not want to break her resolve never to enter the cafeteria again. She had enough money for lunch off campus if only she had a pass.

Suddenly she had an idea: Allan could get lunch for her. Would he be at school today, and would she find him in time? Maybe she should ditch Kooner's class and talk to Allan. She had to find a way to deal with that man. If only she had taken American lit at Marlborough. Then he'd be teaching some other required course. Forget Kooner.

The second period ended and she hadn't seen Allan. She just might have to break her resolve; on top of no breakfast, missing lunch would be too much. Already she was hungry. There were twenty minutes before third period. She decided to get an apple from the vending machine.

It was as if everyone else had the same idea, including Allan. "You're never around when I need you, man," she said, joining him in line.

"Say good morning before you start blowing off," he said and grinned.

"Good morning, Allan," she said sweetly. "Do me a favor."

"That's better. What now?"

"Get me a sandwich and an orange juice off campus at lunchtime."

"I'm cutting out at sixth. Can't wait around 'til seventh."

"Maybe I'll ditch Kooner and eat lunch on his time."

"And mine."

"I'll buy you lunch, too. We can talk, OK?"

By the time they got apples the bell rang. "Why don't I give you the money now—"

"No way. Meet me at your locker the end of fifth. We'll go from there."

The rest of Emma's morning was filled with worry and indecision. How could she convince her mother to write a note to get her back into Kooner's class if she ditched today? There would be a thousand questions. Maybe she should eat in the cafeteria, just this once.

Her mind wandered back and forth, refusing to focus on her classwork. She should probably go on to his class and forget—scramble like the rest of them. That thought recalled the scene in the restaurant. The anger she had felt at her father returned.

Suddenly she knew no matter what, *she would never scramble.* She would ditch class and have lunch with Allan to try to find an answer to her dilemma.

Allan was waiting near the classroom door after fifth period.

"Gotta see Wheeler before I leave campus," he said, pulling her along after him.

"What about lunch?"

"Just take a minute. Come on."

They rushed in only to find Mr. Wheeler hurriedly gathering papers. "Wait for me, Allan. I have to take these reports down to the counselors' office. Be right back."

Emma looked around the room. Every inch of chalkboard was covered. Wall space was crowded with posters and pictures, including those of some Black writers. She glanced at the chalkboard again and read aloud, *"An African Proverb: Because we are, I am."*

"You read it wrong." Allan said. "Emphasize the *we,* not the *I: Because* we *are, I am."*

"What difference does it make?" Emma demanded.

"A lot. The *I* is always included in we. *We,* never in I. So the *we* becomes all inclusive. Example: We're all in the same boat."

She looked at Allan. Why does he always have to be so heavy? She recalled the day he had classified the students, and the time he had explained why he had chosen Manning. Her mind flashed to Kooner and the scramble. "And sinking fast," she said angrily.

"Don't write us off."

"I'm not writing people like us off. I'm thinking about those idiots and Kooner." Suddenly she had a glimpse of what Allan meant. In Kooner's room every class Allan had identified was represented: James, the boojei; Carrie, the climber; Liz, the survivor; and lots of toms. This glimmer made her understand the anger and humiliation she had known in that room. She laughed uneasily. "Man, Kooner sure lumps us all together."

"Now you're getting the point. When we *all* get the point, the Kooners of the world will be as useless as a robot without a programmer. *We program* the Kooners."

Emma felt a rush of excitement. What if she told the class what Allan had just said? Maybe they would see the scramble for what it was.

"What's keeping Wheeler?" Allan asked. "We gotta git outta here if we're gonna eat today."

"Allan," Emma cried, "help me. I want to get all of us in Kooner's class together."

"Send them a notice."

"Allan, this has to be a secret."

"Write it in code."

"Great idea! Let's do it." Suddenly she remembered she should be in Kooner's class. She became frightened. What if she were caught in Wheeler's room alone with Allan. She would be in serious trouble. "We gotta get out of here, Allan. I'm ditching."

"OK, OK, I'll leave Wheeler a note and see him later."

It was easy to get lost on the crowded yard. Emma was anxious to get the notices started. The whole process had to be completed in minimum time, with minimum risk. They had only three hours to come up with a plan to get the students to a meeting and arrange it so that even they would not guess what the meeting was about. "Allan, should we start out with something like ... er ... 'It's a matter of dignity and destiny'?"

"Then they sho' won't show." Allan laughed. "How do they look at scrambling?"

"It's fun and games."

"So, you gotta meet them where they at, woman. The last thing you want to do is make them look stupid. Now, let's think *who, what, where,* and *when.*"

"We want just sixth period from Room 202, to talk, under the bonsai tree, tomorrow."

They quickly came up with five lines:

> Just you in sixth, Room 202,
> Come talk under the bonsai tree.
> Talk of fun and games
> Tomorrow at eighth.
> Don't be late.

"Allan, that doesn't sound right. Something is missing. We gotta say at least one word about the scramble. I can't just come from nowhere with it."

"Keep thinking."

"I am. I'm thinking the whole thing is too big a gamble."

"Hey, you got it," Allan shouted. "Let's put it together."

They finished the note and suddenly realized they needed thirty-five copies. "We'll have to find a copying machine," Emma said.

"That means money."

"We'll give up lunch," Emma said.

Seventh period was almost over when Allan returned with thirty-five clean copies. Emma read aloud:

> Just you in sixth, Room 202,
> Come talk under the bonsai tree.
> Talk of fun and games,
> Talk of gambling with scrambling,
> Tomorrow at eighth.
> Please, don't be late.

Excitedly they divided the chore. Emma gave notices to the girls, Allan gave them out to the boys.

In the hallway as classrooms emptied, the task was difficult. However, on the grounds, where only a few people were still eating lunch, Emma found the going easier. Liz was with Brenda and their little group in their territory. Emma handed Liz a notice.

Brenda quickly snatched the paper. "What's this mess?"

"Stop, Bren. Gimme that," Liz screamed.

"Lemme see what it is." Brenda held on.

"It's none of your business, Brenda. Give it back to Liz," Emma said firmly.

"Ha! Listen whose tryin' t' tell me what t' do. I'll tear the shit up."

Emma, controlling her rage, spoke softly, "Tear it up and I promise, you'll never tear up anything else."

There was sudden silence. Emma moved in on Brenda. "Go on, tear it." She stared Brenda in the eye as the silence deepened. "Tear it up," she almost whispered.

Brenda broke the stare and handed the paper to Liz.

Emma waited, feeling she would not be hassled by Brenda again. Finally she said, "I hope you'll be there, Liz."

"She won't," Brenda muttered.

"That's up to Liz." As Emma walked away she heard Brenda caution Liz angrily. "If you do go, don't count y'self no friend o' mine."

The anger Emma had felt when she moved to dare Brenda turned to hurt. Why had she thought she could work with people who would do something like scrambling for books. She should have had lunch instead of wasting money on copying notices. Maybe none of them would show.

Right on time Allan returned with all notices delivered. "I wouldn't do this for nobody but you, Em."

She told him what had happened with Brenda. "All this could be for nothing."

"No way. In this one, Em, if you *lose*, you win. Think about it."

She hugged him around the waist. "I'll make up the lost lunch. Bring you one tomorrow made with my own hands."

She went to meet her mother, wishing she could feel as assured as Allan that what she had started was a winner no matter what.

"Well, how'd it go today?" her mother asked.

"Fine." She thought of the last couple of hours and wanted to place her head on her mother's lap and cry. Instead, she forced a smile and said, "Just fine."

Nineteen

The house was quiet, Emma's mother sleeping, as Emma finished sandwiches, washed apples and grapes, and wrapped huge slices of homemade gingerbread for tomorrow's lunch.

Then she hurriedly typed a note excusing her absence from Kooner's class on a page from a pad— *Note From the Desk of Janet Walsh.* Why not? she told herself. How many times had Kooner, while searching through piles of papers for a lost note, told students, "Write another; you know you wrote that one." He was forever losing or misplacing things.

She went over the freshly typed pages of her speech, pleased that it was taking shape. She had done all she could do right then for she had not completed all of the research. Still, she put off going to bed. She rolled her hair, put away things strewn around, cleaned out her purse, and laid out clothes for the morning.

How she hated to face tomorrow. What if somebody showed the notice to Kooner and he came? The thought made her shiver. Maybe she should contact everybody first thing and call it off. He'd still know she had planned it. If she got into trouble, that would be the end—no graduation, no college, no profession. What was she thinking about, getting involved in such a thing?

Finally in bed, she forced herself to lie still, concentrating on sleep, pushing all thoughts of "what if" away.

She awoke startled out of a dream she vaguely remembered. It had something to do with the class booing and chasing her down the hall into Kooner's room. Kooner frightened her more than the students. The clock showed that it was only five o'clock. She lay still, hoping to get another hour of sleep, but her mind was too full of things: the dream, the meeting, her paper. . . .

She was startled awake again. The phone was ringing. Who could it be so early in the morning? It was Gary. She was so excited she squealed with delight when he said he could come down for the prom. When she hung up she thought of Kooner. Maybe she should have told Gary. Then the joy welled up again. "He said, 'yes.'" She hugged herself. Yes, yes, yes!

Bounding around the room, she was glad she had put things under control last night. Now she had plenty of time. There would be no hassle with her mother.

The whole morning went smoothly. The only sign that notices had been given were the secret smiles and friendly *Hey, Em*s from class members on the ground and in the hall. Liz asked if she could bring somebody, and Don wanted to know if money was needed for stakes.

It was not until the scrambling for books went off as usual, however, that Emma breathed a small sigh of relief. Nobody was aware that their idea of fun and games was threatened. With that minimum of assurance, she joined Allan for lunch. Before she settled, she told him about the friendliness of everyone and how Kooner suspected nothing and moved right into the scramble. They even got some work done, but not much.

She watched Allan eat, wishing she had as good an appetite. She was nervous, on edge. Would they come? If they came, what would she say?

"Are you gonna meet with us, Allan?"

"Would love to, but I'm not in Room 202 at sixth. It wouldn't look cool if I showed."

"I need you. I don't know what I'll say, even."

"Let them do some talking."

"And I just steer, eh?"

"Right. Guide it the way it should go."

"You make it sound so easy."

"You just have to know for sure what you want to happen, stay loose, and let others help you make it happen."

Allan left her under the bonsai tree just before eighth period began. He promised to wait for the outcome in the library.

Emma waited. She tried to empty all thoughts from her mind so that she could fill it with words that would bring her classmates onto her side. Suddenly she realized that she didn't want to put Kooner down; she only wanted the students to see scrambling for what it was. She also wanted them to help Kooner know that scrambling was wrong, and that they were not going to participate any more. She remembered that while looking at a catalog from Howard University she had read a statement from a former dean: *"It is not the treatment of a people that degrades them, but their acceptance of it. . . ."*

"Where's everybody?" Carrie said, interrupting Emma's thoughts.

"They'll be here," Emma said with assurance.

They did come, on time, all except Liz. Emma waited a few minutes, then went to the point.

"What?" someone shouted and they all started talking at once.

"I thought this was about fun and games," someone sneered.

Some laughed derisively when they knew there was to be no real gambling.

Emma saw Liz slip quietly into the group. Her courage was renewed. "Please, wait . . ." she cried.

"Yeah, shut up," Carrie said.

"At least listen to the lady," Don muttered.

"It's a real gamble," Emma said. "Let's bet that we will outsmart Kooner, call his bluff, say we won't scramble and win."

"Who you think'll tell Kooner we aren't gonna scramble no more?" James asked.

"You always flapping your lips 'round Kooner. You tell 'im," Walt said.

"We can all tell him and not say a word." Emma tried to get back to the point.

"Naw, I don't think we should try that. Mr. Kooner ain't lame, you know," James countered.

"He sho' ain't bright, neither," Liz muttered and everybody laughed.

"He might be very bright," Emma said, "but I think he should have figured out by now that we need only *one* more book."

"We need thirty-five books," James countered again.

"She don't know what she talkin' 'bout." Someone agreed with James.

"James, you just mad 'cause it ain't your idea," Don said. "Go on, Emma."

"I know we're already doubled up with only one person always without a book," Emma said.

"If he can't see that and a teacher, he ain't bright." Liz cracked everybody up again.

Emma moved quickly. "So, what do you say? Shall we gamble?"

"I say gamble," Carrie said. "Scurrying for them books ain't fun no more, anyway."

Emma explained the plan. "Remember, it's our secret. Nobody, *but nobody,* is to know except us. Promise!"

"And if any of you feel you're gonna flake out, then ditch tomorrow." Carrie was stern with her advice.

Emma was bursting with excitement when she found Allan. Things were going her way. She had a feeling that the long gamble planned would bring an end to the scramble.

She wrote Gary a note: *I should warn you. I might not get to the prom. . . . So now you see. I put my head under that tiger's paw. If I come out of this alive, I'll be able to face anything—even Stanford.*

Twenty

If Mr. Kooner was surprised at the room being filled shortly after the second bell, he didn't let on. Emma was alert to his every move, every change of expression, looking for any indication that the secret may be out.

In his usual manner Mr. Kooner read announcements. The list today was long and varied: elections for the prom queen and her court were underway; seniors interested in jobs should report to the office; candy drive advanced orders; usher club. . . . Emma worried. Maybe he had learned about the plan and was not going to hold class at all.

The reading went on: field trip for eleventh graders; driver's ed test. Finally a sudden voice change brought Emma to attention. *"Seniors only: All papers for the competition for a speaker's spot at graduation are due in to your teacher for screening the day after tomorrow."*

Emma sighed. Her paper was in good shape; she'd have it finished. If only he'd get on with the scramble. She looked around the room. How were the others feeling? she wondered. Were they as worried and as nervous as she? She dared not look at anyone long enough to catch an eye. She might crack up and ruin the whole plan, she was so jittery.

Finally Mr. Kooner went to the books and paused as if counting them. Had he added one? Emma quickly counted—only eight in one pile and nine in the other. The same. She held her breath.

"Get set, go." The books were on the floor.

Nobody moved. In the silence Emma could hear the accelerated heartbeat in her chest.

Mr. Kooner was caught off guard. "OK, now, get with it." He laughed a short laugh. "We don't have much time."

No one moved.

He seemed confused. Then he became angry. "I guess I'll have to charge you all with insubordination and fail everyone of you."

Emma felt cold sweat running down her arms. Would they hold out against that threat? She stiffened in her seat, trying to ward off the sudden shivering.

Still nobody moved.

She looked up at Mr. Kooner. He caught her eye and suddenly she recognized the look on his face. It was the one she had seen when she first noticed him in the yard with the other teachers. *He was afraid.* Suddenly she realized that he suspected her. She became frightened and felt the urge to run from the room.

"Mr. Kooner." Liz's voice broke the silence. "We ain't goin' move, and all you gotta do is git *one* book." The silence remained.

A gradual change came over Mr. Kooner's face. He seemed more at ease, but said nothing.

Everyone breathed again and sighs were heard around the room. The bell rang and Emma knew Mr. Kooner was as relieved as they. By tomorrow he will have found that one book, she thought.

The students were restrained until they were out of the hall. Then they let loose with laughter, hand slapping, and hugs. They believed they had won. Were they celebrating a victory too soon?

At the sound of the bell, books were passed out —one for every two students and one extra—and the lesson was immediately underway. Sometimes a joke or an unusual mispronunciation of a word brought peals of laughter. However, by and large, everyone was attentive. The teaching was almost formal. Once upon a time, Emma might have been happy with these events in Room 202.

On surface Mr. Kooner appeared pleased with the change, but Emma felt she was coasting in mined waters. Her instinct to flee had been right that day when she had seen the fright on Kooner's face: She had been and still was suspect. It was as though the weapon was poised, waiting for the right moment to strike.

The first sign of hostility was Kooner's benign unawareness of Emma's existence. He never recognized her in class, even if she raised her hand. Though she knew she had done well on all tests and was prepared for the finals, this being ignored made her a bit uneasy.

On the day of the deadline for the speech competition, two days after the gamble on the scramble, Emma turned in her speech to Mr. Kooner. Feeling a sense of pride in her carefully written, neatly typed pages, she approached his desk just before the second bell. He did not look up.

"Mr. Kooner, here's my speech for the competition," she said. Still no response. Emma shrugged, placed the speech on the desk, and sat down.

Days passed and Mr. Kooner said nothing. She felt she had done a good job, but surely there must be some need for revision. Maybe he had not gotten around to reading it.

With graduation only three weeks away, Emma was too involved in senior activities to keep the competition uppermost in her mind. There were pictures to take, measurements for the cap and gown, the excitement of Gary's coming, and the fun of prom night. Then suddenly the day came when the committee would meet to choose the three speakers and three alternates for graduation. Emma did not know what to do, but she wanted to know if her speech would be considered in the final round.

Early that morning Allan was waiting in their usual place. Her first words after greetings were, "Kooner has said nothing about my speech."

"Did you say anything to him?"

"I didn't think I should. He's the critic. I don't feel comfortable asking him what he thinks."

"Ms. Dohling discussed the speeches turned in to her with each one of us. I know I'm in the finals. You better talk to Kooner. They're meeting today."

Emma saw Mr. Kooner near the vending machines. He was close to a group of teachers, but not with the group. When she started toward him, he moved into the group, his back to her.

Why had he turned away? She felt a wave of weakness, a sinking stomach. She did not want to be embarrassed, yet she had to know about her speech. She risked the possibility of being ignored and asked pardon for the interruption. No response.

Finally, one of the teachers in the group nudged Mr. Kooner. "Jack, this young lady wants your attention."

Emma's heart beat wildly and she was flooded with shame.

"What is it?" he asked curtly.

"My paper . . . the speech I turned in. Will it be considered . . . ?"

"Did you give me a speech?"

"Yes, in the room."

"You sure?"

Her shame turned to fright. Had he not seen her speech at all? "Of course, I'm sure."

"Did you hand it to me?"

"I put it on the desk," Emma said, feeling desperate.

A thin smile played on his face. "Oh . . . you should've put in my hands."

All that work, she thought. She felt panicky. "Let's look on your desk."

"I'll check after the first bell. Come by after then."

Emma pushed through the crowd toward Allan, trying to fight the feeling of having been deeply wounded. Why couldn't he look now? Every moment of waiting was like being held forcibly underwater.

Allan tried to reassure her that Kooner would find the speech—all would be well. There were not that many speeches in the competition, and her chances as a speaker or an alternate were more than good.

Still Emma worried. Maybe this was his way of revenge. He had found that one book, led them to think he was not ruffled, and now he would keep her out of the competition. But he couldn't do that, she thought. Why had she waited until the last minute?

The first bell rang. Allan went with her to Kooner's room. Emma was a bit hopeful when she saw the stack of papers on Mr. Kooner's desk, but the search did not produce her speech. Kooner had triumphed.

Emma held back the tears when she told Allan that her speech had been lost. But she walked down the hall weeping, not knowing what to do, trying to force herself to forget it, not really caring.

But why should Kooner triumph? exploded in her mind. "Maybe I can rewrite my speech." She dried her eyes with the back of her hand.

"They're meeting at noon. You wouldn't have time," Allan said.

"I still have the rough draft. I'd only have to type it."

"Where's your rough draft?"

"Oh, Lord. If only I could get home, Allan."

"Call your mother," Allan said excitedly.

Emma pulled Allan along to the office. She was so excited. She would have time to go home, type her speech, and give it directly to the committee when they met at noon. It was now fifteen minutes after eight. She must hurry.

She called her mother at work. She had just missed her. Her mother was out in the field all day. "I *must* reach her," she shouted into the phone. *No way,* was the answer.

What would she do? An adult would have to get her off campus. Maybe her father was still at home. All he had to do was get her to her house. He wouldn't have to wait while she typed. Maybe he'd find a way to get her back—a taxi even.

When she learned that her father had just left home for the hospital, where he would be in surgery all morning, she burst into tears. She could hardly compose herself enough to tell Jody what had happened.

Finally she understood what Jody was saying: "I'll come get you; tell me where you are."

She was so relieved she clung to Allan right in the office and let the tears flow. "This is my lucky day," she said through tears. "Jody was about to leave home, too. She has some kind of part-time thing, but she's coming." She looked at Allan and forced a grin.

Just at the beginning of fifth period, Emma handed the guard a note that would let her reenter the school grounds. She pushed through to the hall that led to the meeting room of the committee.

They were just about to enter. "Mr. Wheeler, Ms. Dohling, wait a minute," she shouted. She gave them each a copy of her speech and explained what had happened. She then went past them into the room to give Mr. Kooner a copy also. He had no choice but to take it.

When she reentered the hall there was a burst of cheers: "Emma! Emma! yea, yea, yea." There were Allan and all of the students from Room 202. Carrie and Liz hugged her. She was happy that they approved of her making the deadline. Now all she had to do was wait for the results.

Twenty-one

The sky was still heavily overcast that June afternoon as the graduation class of Manning High marched into the stadium under the eyes of their families and friends.

Emma was a bit nervous, filled with mixed feelings: happy to be graduating, but sorry to have had so little time with her new-found friends in Room 202, especially Liz and Carrie.

She sat listening to the praise for her class and was surprised, though pleased, that she, too, was moved by the spirit of the occasion. She knew this praise was too little, too late. She was overwhelmed and could not withhold her joy or her tears when Allan was introduced for his speech: Valedictorian, National

Honor Student, National Awards winner, winner of Today's Music Masters Award, and the University of Southern California's Music Scholarship Award. He was on his way. She was proud; he was her friend.

The sun broke through as the next speaker was announced: National Honor student, recipient of the National Merit Award, future student of Stanford University . . . class speaker, *Emma Walsh.*

Emma winked at Allan, rose, and walked determinedly to the podium. She looked out at the vast, applauding crowd and saw her father and Jody. Her mother was beaming; with her mother were Cheryl and Dee. Down front, smiling, sat Gary.

She felt a sudden rush of love, satisfaction, and confidence as she began her speech: "Where Do We Go From Here?" She moved clearly, deliberately, and forcibly through the words that declared her proud to be a Manning Girl, ready to go from this place into an uncertain world, certain that she now had the desire and the will to help make earth a safer and healthier place for *all* living things.